I0653143

OVER GREEN Fields

By

ZAY SEVIER

Copyright © 2013 Zay Sevier
All rights reserved
ISBN: 0615849849
ISBN-13: 978-0615849843

Published by Zay Sevier
Greensboro, North Carolina

Over Green Fields

One

A Stranger

As far as Stephanie could see there was verdant farmland on either side of her, interspersed with plots of open earth. Her car purred along, and the comfortable sound of the motor echoed her own feeling of contentment, as well as the slight tinge of anticipation she felt. It was as if the car were also viewing the landscape and sharing her joy at being here of all places in the world, enjoying the fresh air and surveying the long rows of the green fields. The air was pungent with the smell of new-tilled soil mixed with the tang of growing rice and bean crops.

She was anticipating the end of the journey, which had taken her from St. Louis all the way down into the Delta lands. Stephanie had passed broad cotton and rice fields, and now she recalled that the soybeans she saw were actually a rotation crop, to keep the land fertile and help control erosion. Soon she would come to the end of her trip, which hadn't been tedious on the interstate highway, but now the smaller roads were slowing her down somewhat.

Stephanie knew she would be welcome at her grandmother's house. She remembered exactly how her grandmother looked. A remarkably trusting face, longer than it was wide, her black eyes looking out of gold-rimmed spectacles. In her eyes Stephanie was always able to see a twinkle of humor. But now her grandmother, Eleanor Kimball, was partially confined to a wheelchair--not that she would be slowed down or her spirits dampened in the least.

Stephanie had only been for a visit in the Delta twice since Judson Kimball died some years ago. She remembered her grandmother at the funeral, holding her head high and vowing to "fight Carmichael with her dying breath." It was one of the few times Stephanie had noticed anger in her grandmother. Mrs. Kimball almost blamed Mr. Carmichael, a prominent financial figure in the Delta, for her husband's death by his heavy-handed oppression. At that time Carmichael controlled much of the real estate and farm revenues in the area, and his rise to power had caused, directly and indirectly, the downfall of many hopes and dreams.

But that was all in the past. Now Stephanie's grandmother assured her that she would be more help than bother when she came to stay. There was only a housekeeper to attend to the affairs of the home, and Stephanie would be able to help her grandmother with her crop accounts and other paperwork. And Stephanie was looking forward to helping around the house in many other ways.

She passed several familiar little towns, and she knew Stanley was the next—a city of about fifteen thousand inhabitants—and her grandmother's comfortable farmhouse was another ten or twelve miles beyond that. She glanced down at her gasoline gauge. It registered dangerously near the empty mark. She could probably make it to her grandmother's, but why not play it safe? She was approaching a service station, and she slowed down and pulled in.

There was a sign on the pump that said "Full Service Only," so she waited. And waited. Finally the attendant approached her, at a snail's pace, with one word: "Fill"?

Stephanie saw no reason to hazard the effusiveness of a two-word answer, so she merely smiled and nodded.

The gasoline hose imitated its master in its sluggishness. And added to that was the near-empty level of the tank.

Stephanie unconsciously put her hand to the dashboard to give the car a friendly pat. As the attendant checked the oil level, she thought how lucky she had been to get the car. It was a used car, but had only been used about six months by one of her acquaintances at her father's office, and even then the woman had simply driven it back and forth to the office, about six or seven miles a day. When Stephanie's father died, she had inherited quite a comfortable income from his investments and insurance, and she was the only heir. She knew that her old Saturn wouldn't make the trip into the Delta, and she had offered to buy Mrs. Simpson's car.

It was a beauty. Stephanie patted the dashboard again, and then paid the service station attendant, who then moseyed back to his lounge chair in the station. She turned her key in the dash, expecting to hear the familiar hum of the motor, but the starter kept whirring with no luck.

Stephanie was persistent, but the car simply refused to start. She got out of her seat and went up to the attendant. "I seem to be having trouble starting my car," she said. "Can you help me?"

The attendant squinted at her slightly and pursed his lips. He was silent for a moment, as if considering his answer.

"Well, I don't fix 'em. I just puts gas in 'em." He looked out across the fields on the other side of the road.

"But, I told you I was having trouble. Won't you just . . .?" She saw that he was obviously more interested in the effect of the slight wind that stirred the bean plants across the road than in her dilemma. It was useless to try to talk to him. She returned to the car and again turned the starter, hoping that the car had just needed a rest. Again no luck. She took her cell phone out of her purse.

Suddenly she was aware of a huge black car on the other side of the gas pumps, and a youngish man getting out to go into the station for something. He looked at her briefly, and she felt as if he could see into her most private thoughts.

He had a smooth complexion, and black hair and eyes, which lent him a commanding if somehow roguish appearance. She noticed that as he approached the station, the attendant rose from his chair and made a movement that might have been taken for a tiny bow.

The man's glance had frightened Stephanie, she couldn't explain why. She hoped he wouldn't notice her, because if he did he would almost surely say something to her and for some reason she was terrified at the thought of speaking to him. She found herself holding her breath, as if it would make her less conspicuous.

As the man turned to come out of the station house, Stephanie quit turning the starter and gazed out over the green fields. Perhaps he wouldn't see her. He was almost to his car when he stopped and approached Stephanie.

"I beg your pardon, are you having trouble with your car?"

"Well, yes, I am, but it's nothing. It will start in a few minutes, I'm sure." Stephanie smiled weakly. Her mouth was dry. "Thank you anyway."

She hoped he would go away, even though she knew she ought to ask him to help her. She was at a loss to explain to herself what it was about him that frightened her.

Then his hand was on the car door.

"Get out of the car," he said simply, in a voice that wasn't threatening, but that told her he was accustomed to being obeyed. He opened the door to emphasize his command.

She had no choice but to obey, though what he could hope to do by turning the key in the starter was beyond her. He got into the driver's seat and tried the starter. Stephanie almost felt exultant when the car again wouldn't start. "You will throw your weight around, mister," she thought.

He pulled the hood release and got out of the driver's seat. He had the hood up in a flash, and was looking at the engine. Stephanie could recall seeing her father in the same position many times when she was a child. It was before her father had become so important in the business world, and they had an older model car. She remembered the car fondly. It wasn't what she could call a pretty car, like this one, but it was comfortable. Except when it wouldn't run. At times like that her father would lift the hood and lean in to do something to the spark plugs, or wires—maybe even to the gas supply, and Stephanie would turn the starter, and it would start! How she had admired her father! But he was gone now.

"Get in and try it," the dark man was saying. Stephanie came out of her reverie with a jolt.

She got in the car and turned the key, almost hoping it wouldn't start. He seemed so sure of himself, and it would help her ego to see him taken down a notch. But to her surprise the car started right up. She looked at the man and noticed he still had a stern face, but was now almost smiling to himself, as if to say: "You see, I knew what I was doing all along." He obviously thought of himself as a superior being, without whom the world would be in a sorry mess.

The man let the hood down with a little bang and gave her the kindest, warmest smile she could imagine. It took her quite by surprise, because at this moment he seemed to be as gentle and . . . human, not the arrogant, forbidding person he had first appeared.

"I don't know how to thank you," she said, her hand still resting on the partially open car door. She glanced at his huge, expensive car on the other side of the pump and couldn't think of anything else to say.

He looked at her for an instant with eyes that seemed to indicate that a simple thank you wouldn't be enough. He was obviously enjoying the moment.

"You are a beautiful woman," he said. Do you know that your lips are inviting a kiss?"

"How dare you!" she retorted, putting her had to her mouth. She felt a blush just starting at her hairline.

"There," he said. "Your charming blush proves you're no innocent, and I'll wager you would enjoy a kiss."

Stephanie was at a loss for words. "What nerve! What insolence!" she thought. Still, she couldn't help noticing his sensitive lips and aquiline features, his almost mysterious facial expression made sharper by his lean but muscular build. Her blush deepened against her will.

"I assure you," she spluttered, "I offer my thanks, but you certainly have no right to . . . to suggest such a thing." She glanced up at him as she spoke. His dark eyes, hawkish, were seeking hers, and she could feel the electricity between them.

"So chaste," he said, with a hint of mockery in his voice. "How pleasant. Almost like a breath of fresh air."

He looked at her for another moment and then started back to his own car. Then he stopped and turned back toward Stephanie.

"Do you live around here?" he asked.

After his impertinence, Stephanie wasn't inclined to answer, but again his commanding tone seemed to leave her little choice.

"No, I'm . . . well, yes, I suppose I do, at present." She felt awkward at her reply.

"You had better have this," he said, fishing in his breast pocket for a piece of paper. He wrote something on it and handed it to Stephanie. "If you have any more trouble, just call. Ask for Max."

She was puzzled. Gone was the self-assured manner, the egotism, and it seemed replaced by a warmth, a friendly sincerity.

When the man had gone, Stephanie thought about her encounter with him. She hated his type. He was so arrogant. He took everything for granted, and the most unendurable irony was that his kind of man always seemed to get what he wanted.

And yet there was an undeniable current that had passed between them. She had never felt like this under a man's gaze before. It was as if his voice and his eyes were able to make contact with her very soul.

"Max," she said aloud, and the name hung in the air, sounding strange to her ears. He could have been a figment of her imagination, except that here she sat with her car running and a blush still tingling on her face. And the car definitely wouldn't start before.

She looked over at the service station attendant. He was still gazing out across the bean fields as she drove off.

Two

Stephanie

Eleanor Kimball's house looked almost exactly as Stephanie remembered it, with vines on the lattice porch and wide steps flanked by oleander bushes. The whole aspect of the house was conditioned by the huge shady elm that dominated the front yard.

Stephanie pulled into the driveway and brushed her shoulder-length brown hair off her neck. It was cooler here in the shade of the elm, and as she stepped out of the car, she looked around the side of the house. The sight of the old sweet gum tree in the back brought back memories of the tire swing that had hung from its branches.

Stephanie Gray was of medium height, and her brown eyes complemented her hair. As a general rule her olive complexion didn't require much more than a small amount of makeup, with an almost natural shade of lipstick. Her chin was dimpled, which gave her face a slightly more youthful appearance than her twenty-three years.

Her step quickened as she approached the front door. She expected her grandmother to answer the bell, but instead a robust and healthy-looking girl of about seventeen or eighteen came to the door.

"You must be Betsy," said Stephanie.

"And you're Stephanie?" asked the other with a beaming face. She spontaneously gave Stephanie a little hug, polite but natural and almost maternal. Then she took the overnight bag from Stephanie and led the way into the house.

Stephanie was cheered by Betsy's congeniality. She straightened the collar of the violet cotton blouse she had worn for the trip. "Is grandmother here?" she asked.

"Yes, she is," answered Betsy. "She was taking a nap earlier, but I think I heard her stir a few minutes ago. These late summer afternoons get a little too tiring for her these days. Just make yourself at home while I check on Miss Eleanor and tell her you're here." She gave Stephanie another smile and went up the long staircase.

Stephanie looked around. The house hadn't changed much since she had been here. The staircase on the left side of the foyer seemed to lend an air of grandeur to the room. She looked on the other side of the foyer into the living room. Her favorite chair was still there beside the tall bookcase, and the room still seemed to command quiet. One expected to speak in a hushed voice when in the living room, as in a library. The expensive-looking rug was made more elegant by the highly polished oak floor peeking out from its edges, and the two beautifully decorated lamps set the tone for the rest of the furnishings.

She went on down the rather wide vestibule, past the staircase and elevator, and into the kitchen.

As she passed the elevator, she heard the faint clank that announced someone on the way down. Her grandfather had installed the elevator when it became too difficult for Mrs. Kimball to climb the long stairs, even with her cane. Stephanie remembered the restrictions against her using the elevator except when she went up or down with her grandmother. It seemed like only yesterday that her grandmother had been walking around, as spry as could be, only using her cane in the afternoons or when they went to town.

Stephanie was fifteen at the time, and she remembered the bitterness she had felt when her mother died. She was bitter against the whole world, because somehow she blamed the world for taking her mother away from her. So when she went to live with the Kimballs for the year following her mother's death, she brooded for several weeks. Her grandparents understood, and left her alone.

They had learned to square their chins in the face of adversity. Stephanie's grandfather had told her how more than once he had lost his entire crop—a year's work—owing to inadequate flood control. And now they had lost their daughter, but they were still able to get over their grief and give comfort to Stephanie.

With her grandparent's help she had finally come out of her dismal state of mind and begun to face the world with a renewed spirit, to value life for what it is instead of what it might have been.

The elevator door opened, and there sat Mrs. Kimball with a smile on her face.

"There's my girl," she said.

"Oh, Grandmother," said Stephanie, bending down into a warm hug. "Let me look at you. Why, you look younger than you did last time I was here."

"Nonsense," said Mrs. Kimball. "I'm getting older just like everybody else is. But I'm the same cantankerous woman I always was. Now let's go into the kitchen. I hope you're hungry, because I understand Betsy is planning a dinner that will melt in your mouth."

She turned to Betsy. "I have to brag on Betsy. She is about the best cook in the county." She smiled at the young housekeeper, who was so overcome with pride that she closed her eyes in a broad grin. "She's been with me a little over a year now, and she can't be beat."

Mrs. Kimball rolled herself in the chair. "I don't need this darn chair all the time. In fact, I usually walk, using my old cane. But sometimes it's a little slow going."

She suddenly stopped her chair and looked up to Stephanie. "Why Stephanie, I believe you're almost as big as a grown woman. How old are you now, child?"

"Now Grandmother, you know I'm twenty three. I think you had better become accustomed to the idea that I <u>am</u> a grown woman, not the little girl you used to hold on your lap." Stephanie sipped the tea Betsy had handed her.

Betsy was going on about her cooking, and Stephanie felt she should help, but when she suggested it, her grandmother just shook her head.

"No, Betsy just wants us to stay out of her way for now. There will be plenty of time for that later. Right now let's go into the living room."

Stephanie wheeled her in, and sat in her favorite chair facing her grandmother.

"I saw your old friend Nola in town the other day," began Mrs. Kimball. "You remember her, she use to have tight ringlets all over her head when she was a teenager. Now she has let her hair grow out and it is just beautiful to behold."

"Of course I remember her," said Stephanie. "We write occasionally. She did wear ringlets, didn't she? But I always admired her for the luscious honey-golden color of her hair."

"She's working in the office of the Stanley weekly," said Mrs. Kimball. "She lays out displays, whatever that means."

"Oh, that means she designs the layout of the display ads—the large ads for the paper. I suppose she works with the advertiser and writes copy for the ads--that sort of thing. I'm sure there's a lot more to it than that, but essentially she prepares the material for the computer. What did she have to say?"

"I can't remember everything she said, but she was happy to learn you were coming here to stay." Mrs. Kimball gave Stephanie an apprehensive glance. "She also said she was engaged to be married."

"Oh, you don't say! What delightful news! Has she set a date?"

"She didn't tell me about that, but she certainly seemed happy."

"Who is she engaged to?"

"I've been trying to remember his name. Maybe you know him—he's that handsome boy with black hair."

Stephanie's thoughts immediately went to the man she had seen at the service station—Max. He was handsome in a craggy sort of way, now that she thought about it. She was afraid to say his name, almost as if she didn't want to face it if Nola were engaged to him.

Mrs. Kimball noticed the disconcerted look on her face. "You probably don't know him anyway," she said. "Oh, I remember his name now—it's Jeff. Jeff Kern."

"Jeff Kern? Of course I remember him. He was a nice enough boy, but I thought he was too interested in his horses to ever notice anybody like Nola, as cute as she was. I guess it's a crazy world." She laughed a little nervous laugh and was surprised to realize that she was relieved it wasn't Max. His name sprang to her lips and she was on the verge of asking her grandmother about him, but then thought better of it.

"What about yourself, Stephanie? I suppose there are boys back in St. Louis who are very disappointed that you've moved. Is there anyone you're interested in?"

"No, I don't have anyone. I haven't lived a reclusive life—you can't do that in a city like St. Louis—but I just haven't found anyone I could be serious about."

"Well, I'm afraid you won't find any of the young men around here to be very interesting," said Mrs. Kimball. An impish smile lighted her face. "But there is hope. I seem to see new faces every time I go to town."

"Oh, Grandmother, I'm not really interested in romance now, anyway. I want my life to settle down a little first."

"I suppose we'll have to talk about what you are going to do, now that your father is gone," said Mrs. Kimball. "You're welcome to stay here as long as you want, and I hope you will stay a long, long time. It won't cost you a penny, either. You know your grandfather left me fairly well off, even though . . ." A dark look came over her brow. ". . . even though our property was almost all taken from us by that low snake. I'm talking about Carmichael."

She gave Stephanie a sharp glance. "Maybe you don't remember. It was Irwin Carmichael who almost literally drove your grandfather to despair and to his grave." She spoke between clenched teeth.

Yes, I remember the name," said Stephanie. "What did he do?"

Her grandmother sighed. "I don't like to talk about it, but I suppose you ought to know. We bought this house and property—including the northeast farmland—from Carmichael.

"That was before your mother came along. Everything went along fine. We had a large farm, producing money crops all the time. Actually we had what amounts to two farms. The west acreage was for reserves.

"During off years we offset our losses on a poor yield by planting soybeans the next season. Well, we had two bad years—in fact it was a couple of years before your mother died. Your grandfather went to Carmichael to plead with him to let us delay payments on our mortgage. He said all right, he would let us have six months. But he was going to charge us a penalty of eight percent on the arrears.

"Well, it was unreasonable, but your grandfather agreed, because there was nothing else we could do. Carmichael controlled all the financial institutions in the area. Not legally, but he had some hold over everyone who had any money at the time.

"I don't know if you want to hear all this, Stephanie. It's all over with now, anyway."

"Please, Grandmother—I do want to know the truth."

"I can only give you my side of it, child. You see, when we first moved here, I knew Estelle Carmichael slightly. As far as I knew, she was a fine woman. But it wasn't long before everyone knew that Irwin was seeing someone else, a woman named Doreen. Doreen had quite a . . . reputation. She was a grasping, avaricious woman, and she had latched onto Irwin Carmichael, mainly because he had a lot of money.

"Finally Estelle could take it no longer, and she left Irwin. I remember she stayed in a rooming house on the other side of Stanley for a little while.

But it was just a few days after Estelle left Irwin that Doreen moved in with him.

"Several people saw Estelle and tried to convince her to take legal action, but she wanted to wash her hands of the whole affair. She said she didn't want any of Irwin's money—tainted money, as she called it.

"So she moved away after a few weeks. It would have been easy for her to get a divorce, but for some reason she didn't. As far as I know, she moved back to Memphis to be with her family.

"In the meantime, Doreen and Irwin became the scourge of Stanley. Doreen had a lot of dirt about many of the most respected men in the area, and Irwin used that to his advantage.

"You see, back in those days Stanley wasn't growing like it is now, but it was a pretty busy town because it was a sizable railroad terminal. Doreen used to have her . . . apartment over Wilson's bar, which was two or three doors down from Carmichael's office in the Cotton Exchange building.

"Carmichael held his own sort of court in a back room at Wilson's bar, and from there he literally ran the town. Wilson always toadied to him. And it was inevitable that the kind of dirt Carmichael was would be attracted to Doreen, especially when he saw how he could use her.

"So times were tough for everyone except Carmichael and his clique. Your grandfather tried to float a loan in Memphis, but he couldn't do it, because Carmichael held the mortgage on so much of his property.

"It wasn't long after our bargain for the delay that Carmichael came here to the house. He had changed his mind, and he said he had to have the mortgage payment plus the penalty. We argued with him, and he got real nasty. He said he would foreclose if we didn't pay up. So we said we would sell him some of our other farm land to make up the mortgage payment.

"Carmichael got a devilish gleam in his eye, and pulled a paper out of his coat pocket. 'You're too late,' he said. 'I already own your west acreage.' It was the soybean farm, the only thing we had to fall back on.

"'What do you mean?' said your grandfather. 'I bought that land from Robert Fisher. I pay him quarterly on my note, and I'll have a clear deed in about six years.'

"'No you won't,' said Carmichael. 'I bought . . . well, acquired all of Fisher's property rights and outstanding mortgages. Here's the note on that acreage.'

"We were both speechless.

"'But I can be generous,' he said. 'I'll pay your entire mortgage for the year—including the penalty you owe—for a quit-claim deed to these west farm lands.'

"We didn't have any choice but to give him our farmlands. The acreage was worth twice as much as he allowed on it, but we were already in debt, not just to him but to several other people in the area."

Mrs. Kimball grew silent.

"So that's why you've always said that he stole your land," said her granddaughter.

"Yes. Your grandfather began to sink from that minute. And it wasn't long before he was in his grave.

"Now Irwin Carmichael has died, and everybody around here can breathe easier. He died without ever doing a kind deed in his life. We had paid him off several years ago, thank God. Doreen left him after she had been with him about a year— went off with a salesman from South Dakota. Carmichael didn't have any children, and I don't know what happened to his properties. I believe they are still tied up in probate court."

"What about his wife?"

"She came from a well-to-do family in Memphis, but I don't know if she is even still alive. She was a dark, frail beauty when she lived here, and she was in her fifties then."

"You still have your farm, don't you, Grandmother? I know you don't work it yourself."

"No, I don't have a farm anymore, except for the land that Bob Bevis has under cultivation. It's a sort of tenant relationship whereby he works the land for a percentage of the profits. I'm pretty comfortably off now, though. Your grandfather and

I had a good insurance policy, and my expenses are few."

At that moment they heard a silvery peal from a bell in the kitchen. Stephanie recognized it of old as the way dinner was called in the Kimball household.

"We can talk more over dinner," said Mrs. Kimball, as Stephanie wheeled her into the dining room.

The dinner proved to be delicious. Mrs. Kimball hadn't exaggerated Betsy's culinary talents at all. During the dessert Mrs. Kimball fixed her eye on Stephanie.

"I want to hear all about my girl now. What have you been doing all these years?" She gave Stephanie a reproachful look.

"Now Grandmother, you know I would have been to see you more often if I could, but I've been involved in so many things I just hadn't the time.

"Before I got out of school, I decided I needed to have a job of some sort, so I asked my father. Since he was a vice president of Triangle Cartons, he suggested I try for one of the vacancies there. The personnel office was impressed with my skills and my attitude, and I went to work in one of the offices. I did some typing and filing, and helped with the hourly wage statements. Sometimes they put me in the front office as a receptionist.

"It was a very pleasant job, and I got along well with just about everyone there. The work was a little tedious, but altogether not too boring. I didn't see Dad all the time, because his office was way on the other side of the building. But often we would have lunch together."

"But then why did you quit Triangle Cartons? You didn't stay very long, and you never told me what led you to quit."

"It wasn't because I didn't like the job. There was a man in the shipping department named Leon—Leon Ainsworth—who was continually chasing me. Actually I liked him pretty well. He finally persuaded me to . . . well, Grandmother, he gave me an engagement ring."

Her Grandmother remained silent.

"It all happened so fast I didn't have time to sort things out. It's just a good thing I realized in time that I didn't love him, and broke off with him.

"I just couldn't stay at Triangle after that, and I applied at Chariton Products for a similar position, and I've been there ever since. When Dad passed away last year, I began to think that maybe I just wasn't cut out to be a receptionist and secretary all my life. You know Dad has lots of investments, and I have a sizable income from them. So when you wrote me to come down, it was the very thing I needed to get away from the big city for a while. I've put most of my things in storage and the house is on the market. I suppose I'll miss the city life a little, but I don't have any more real ties there."

"You're welcome to stay here as long as you like," said her grandmother. "And you don't have to do anything to earn your keep. This house runs just like clockwork, with Betsy around. Isn't she a sweet one?"

"Yes, she must be a great help to you. She and I seem to get along well, too."

The Kimball household retired early. Stephanie had her old bedroom with the bookcase built in the wall. When she went up after dinner she noticed a large portrait of her grandfather on the wall. It brought back how the old man had been so kind to her and companionable when she really needed it. It was almost as if the portrait were there to remind her that every one she had ever loved, except her grandmother, was gone. A little shiver shook her as she realized she was essentially alone in the world now. And she had to be strong for her grandmother's sake.

Stephanie turned to comb out her hair, and as she looked in the mirror on the dressing table she saw that her face was a face of character, character she hadn't noticed in herself until now. She was truly not a little girl anymore—the little girl who had looked in this same mirror so many times was gone long ago. In her place was a woman, and as she saw herself now she knew she was an attractive woman. Perhaps the mirror was telling her something she had never learned from her mirror in St. Louis.

And why had she left St. Louis? She looked into the mirror in vain for the answers to that question. Certainly she wanted to leave behind all her memories of Leon Ainsworth.

But there were other reasons she had to leave St. Louis, reasons she wasn't able to put into thoughts or words yet. They involved her own image of herself. In St. Louis the mirror had shown her only the Stephanie who went to work every day, who did her makeup, who arranged her clothing for the best effect, who fixed her hair one way or the other.

Involuntarily her fingers closed around the hair brush on the dressing table. She was seeing a different Stephanie now, a Stephanie who had escaped from that image she had of herself which was exactly detailed in her mirror. Now it was as if the image in the mirror had blurred outlines, as if she were opening a cocoon and wasn't sure what would emerge. The image was of a beautiful woman, but that was only a physical assurance. All the rest—the personality underneath the surface— was shrouded in questions.

In St. Louis Stephanie had felt as if she were constantly brooding over her father's death. He had been in his prime when he died. He was forty nine years old and was next in line to be president of Triangle Cartons. He was essentially a happy man. After his wife died of pneumonia he took a year to readjust. That was why he sent Stephanie to live with the Kimballs. But after his year spent in introspection, he faced the world with a new purpose. He would never marry again. He thought of Adele Gray as the perfect woman, and no one could ever take her place. Besides, he had Stephanie to look after then, and he was extremely busy with his work.

Stephanie picked up a hair brush from the dressing table. It was the old brush she had used so long ago, the brush her grandmother had given her when she stayed here before. On the back of the brush was a bas-relief in metal of a woman from the Second Empire in full skirts. How Stephanie had dreamed of being like her, with a trim waist and a rather low-cut dress, made even more alluring by the hoop skirt. She looked at her waist in the mirror. Standing here with only her slip on and her shoulders bare, she was transported back to those long indolent days when she was fifteen. Her breasts were full and her waist was trim now, like the girl on the brush, but she knew that even so she was dreaming an idle dream. The days of romance were gone, when perhaps a musketeer or dragoon from the Imperial army would make a low bow to her and with a nod of his head suggest they take a turn on the floor to the strains of a waltz by Johann Strauss.

Those days were gone forever. So were the idle days when she was fifteen, when she had dreamed about how a handsome stranger would someday take her in his arms and declare his undying love to her. When a handsome stranger had come along, in the person of Leon Ainsworth, she had found that it was only for selfish reasons that he had spoken tender words to her. Yes, she had been attracted to him, but he had made love to her only in order to gain a hold on her, to further his own selfish schemes.

The clock in the hall downstairs was striking ten, and it brought Stephanie back to the present with a jolt. She slipped between the clean, crisp sheets, and only then did she realize how tired she was. As she drifted off, another handsome stranger's face appeared to her: it was the man at the service station—Max.

Breakfast was early at the Kimball house. Stephanie decided, with her grandmother's urging, to go into town and see her friend Nola. Nola had told Mrs. Kimball that she wanted Stephanie to have lunch with her the first time she could get to town, and there was no reason she couldn't go today.

Her grandmother's house was on a county road, some six or eight miles from the highway into Stanley. In all the trip was sixteen miles. There was a shortcut, but Stephanie decided to go on the main highway until she was more sure of the area.

Life in Stanley was bustling, even for a small town. The largest street in the business district ran parallel to the highway, one block away. Stephanie parked her car at the parking island in the middle of the broad street, and went over to the newspaper offices.

"I'd like to see Nola Henson," she said to the gray-haired lady in the reception area. The lady was called Mrs. Parker, according to the name plate on the wide counter that separated her work area from the entranceway. Mrs. Parker smiled with one side of her mouth and tilted her head to look at Stephanie over her spectacles.

"Just go right down that hall," she said, pointing to a door marked <u>Employees</u> <u>Only</u>. "It's the first door on the right."

Stephanie followed her directions, and soon found herself in a small office with several drafting tables and a wide desk.

Behind the desk sat her friend Nola. Stephanie recognized her immediately by her dimples. Her cute friend from so long ago had grown into a very attractive woman.

"Do you know me, Nola?" said Stephanie, with a little smile.

"Why, it's Stephanie Gray! I never would have known you if I hadn't been expecting you. How you've changed."

"That much?" asked Stephanie.

"Well, sure. I suppose eight—let's see, is it eight or nine years?—can change a person a lot. And when you consider we were only teenagers then." Nola crinkled her eyes in a tiny grin. "Do you remember how we used to hang on the phone for hours, talking about all the boys in school?"

"You've changed too," said Stephanie, giving Nola a little hug. She leaned back and looked at her friend. "But tell me. Is it true that you are going to be married?"

"Nola held out her left hand for Stephanie to admire the ring on her finger. "I'll tell you about it

over lunch. You will come with me to lunch, I
hope?"

"Of course."

The two went across the street to the Stanley
Café for a "home style" meal. Nola told Stephanie
all about her job at the Stanley Weekly.

"Mrs. Parker is a nice woman—you saw her
in the reception room. She's overly curious, that's
all. Some would call her a busybody, but she's not
really a bad sort if you get to know her. I almost
think she knew I was to be engaged before I did!"
Nola laughed, and Stephanie saw that she kept
glancing at the door.

Nola and Stephanie talked about life in
Stanley, and about the people they had known as
teenagers. "But Stephanie," said Nola, "what about
your job? You seemed to be so happy at—was it
Chariton Products? You haven't written since . . .
well, six or eight months now. Why would you
want to move away from St. Louis?"

It was the very question Stephanie had hoped
Nola wouldn't ask. If she was unable to sort it out
for herself, she couldn't hope to make anyone else
understand, even as close a friend as Nola had been
over the years. Probably, she mused, Nola would
have to stand in her shoes in front of that mirror in
order to understand.

"I just . . . want to get away from the big city
for a while. I kept meeting myself coming back, if
you know what I mean. And I was getting tired of

the same old job all the time, seeing the same people day after day."

Nola nodded in understanding.

Stephanie changed the subject. "About you and Jeff, now. How excited you must be. When is the date?"

"We thought we'd wait until after the end of the year, for various reasons."

Nola sighed. "You know," she continued, "I almost envy you, Stephanie. You don't have any ties anywhere, you can live in the city if you want to. But don't get me wrong. I'm very much in love with Jeff, it's just that . . . well, he's so devoted to his farm and his cattle and horses, he could never think about leaving here." She shrugged her shoulders. "But if that's what he wants, I'll be right at his side. He's the only man who could ever make me happy."

Stephanie's thoughts again went to the man she had seen at the service station. Max. She had to admit to herself that she was intrigued. Max who? Nola would probably know.

"Here he is now," said Nola. Stephanie almost jumped, and turned to see a very handsome dark-haired man come in the door. Jeff Kern, obviously. He had a trim figure and cutting black eyes. As he came up to the table Stephanie noticed two people with him, a man about her own age and a girl evidently in her late teens.

The table was large, and the newcomers all sat down. Nola made the introductions. "You've heard me talk about Stephanie before, Jeff."

"Jeff shook Stephanie's hand and smiled.

"And this is Jeff's sister, Janie, and Marv—Marv Woods."

Stephanie remembered Janie as a girl of seven or eight. She smiled at the trio, and noticed that Marv was looking at her intently. It was almost a stare, and Stephanie hoped she was the only one to notice it.

"It's been a long time, Jeff," Stephanie said, "but I remember you and your horse—Crazy was his name."

"I suppose it really has been a long time, if I had Crazy then," said Jeff with a laugh. I'm surprised you remember him."

"You and that horse were inseparable, if I'm not mistaken. So if I remember you, I'd have to remember him."

Marv spoke up. "Are you from around here originally, then?" he asked.

"Well, no. I suppose it's a long story. I lived her for about a year and a half, some years ago." She noticed that Janie was looking daggers at Marv. "I've lived in St. Louis most of my life, though."

"So you're just here on a visit?"

"No, I've moved in with my grandmother, Eleanor Kimball. I don't have any imminent plans to leave."

Janie appeared to take an interest. "So, the big city girl, come to sample the country life. You won't like it."

"Of course she will," interjected Nola. "Stephanie happens to be one of my very best friends, and I know she likes it here. I can remember the times we had together," she said to Stephanie. She crinkled her eyes and giggled a little, just like she had in the old days. It brought laughter from Stephanie.

"I hate to break this up," said Jeff, "but I have to get back. I just came to town for some parts for that tractor."

Nola's lunch break was over, and she walked to the door with Jeff. Stephanie could tell she had been hoping he would show up.

"They make quite a pair, don't they?" she remarked to Marv and Janie. Marv nodded, but Janie made a tiny petulant expression which Stephanie chose to ignore.

Stephanie was cheered by meeting her friend again. She had some shopping to do in town, and as she put her packages in the car she thought how pleasant it was to have such a warm reception by people in Stanley--excepting Janie, of course.

Janie is probably just intimidated by big city types, and I don't really blame her, she thought. She'll come around in time, when she finds out I'm not an ogre.

Nola had certainly chosen a handsome man. Marv was very good looking too, in a different way than Jeff. A little shorter than Jeff, and with curly dark blond hair. He seemed interested in Stephanie, and Janie didn't like it at all.

Stephanie was in an adventurous mood, and she decided to take the county roads back home, instead of the highway. Once she turned onto the road leading out of town, it all seemed to come back to her, since she had been over these roads many times with her grandfather.

Three

Unpleasant Episode

It was a pleasant drive back toward home, thought Stephanie, as her car whizzed along at a relaxed pace. She hadn't been out of Stanley more than five or six miles when, going around a long curve, she noticed just beyond a stand of trees some orange flowers beside the road, tall and proud, waving in the wind. She slowed down and pulled her car over to the shoulder to admire them. There must be thousands of them, she thought. I'll just take a few home to Grandmother for the dinner table.

She gathered up eight or ten of the long-stemmed Indian paintbrushes. But when she got back to her car, it wouldn't start again. It acted the same way it had at the service station the day before. At least someone had been there to help. If only she could lift the hood and pull a bit of magic the way Mr. Max somebody-or-other had done. And since she had discovered her cell phone had no signal in Stanley, she had left it at home.

Now she could only see rice fields and, further away, a bean field. Then she noticed a rather tumble-down shack just ahead, almost surrounded by long rows of beans. Maybe someone lived there who could help her.

As she walked up to the shack, Stephanie wondered if it was inhabited. It looked deserted, and her heart sank. Then she saw a light bulb burning on the porch. Odd, she thought, for the porch light to be burning right in the middle of the day. But surely someone was about.

She knocked at the door, a little timidly at first, then, fearing the place actually was abandoned, more urgently. She had hardly finished knocking the second time when the door opened a crack and a face peered up at her. It was the face of an old man, white-haired, who had a five-day growth of whiskers. Stephanie thought his eyes were a little wild and distrustful.

"What is't ye want?" he said in a thick brogue.

"I beg your pardon," Stephanie said, "my car has stalled." She gestured toward her car, a quarter of a mile down the road.

The man didn't look in the direction of her car, but kept staring at her in the same malevolent way. It unnerved Stephanie, and she suddenly felt perspiration on her brow.

"It's my car," she said again. "It won't run."

The man bent his head slightly to look at her car, still keeping the door almost shut. "I see that," he said, fixing his eyes on her again. "Well, and what of it?"

"I was hoping you could . . . you could help me." She glanced around apprehensively, vainly hoping she could see some other form of life on the broad horizon so she wouldn't have to continue to fence words with this unpleasant man.

"And what would ye be havin' me do," he replied, "carry y' to town on me back?" His lips parted slightly and Stephanie saw his long pointed teeth in a leering grin.

"Oh, no!" She realized she sounded shocked, which was probably what he wanted, but she didn't care. "I only though perhaps you knew how to make my car run."

Instantly the man put back his head and bellowed, "Jerry!" Then he slammed the weather-beaten door shut again, leaving Stephanie standing on his rickety porch, wondering if she had been dreaming.

She didn't hear a sound within the house, and couldn't decide whether to knock again or abandon all thoughts of the old man's help and begin walking. She tentatively put her hand up with the idea of knocking again, ever so lightly, when the door opened suddenly and she was confronted by a younger man, evidently the man named Jerry. He also had a five-day growth on his face, but his hair was dark brown. His eyes gave Stephanie the impression that he had either been drinking heavily or had just been awakened from sleep.

Stephanie was a little surprised at his sudden appearance. He licked his upper lip and looked at her figure from top to bottom. "Well, where's your car?" he asked.

"It's right down here," she said as cheerfully as she was able, stepping carefully off the porch. "I want to thank you for coming to my rescue. This car has been temperamental lately. I don't know what I would do without somebody to help. I don't know very many people around here, and it's a long way to town." She wasn't thinking about what she said, just talking to keep down her nervousness. The man didn't say anything as they walked along, but simply gave her an indolent half-smile.

When they approached the car, the man reached his hand out for the keys. He got into the driver's seat and turned the starter over several times. "It won't start," he said.

Stephanie thought he probably expected a bravo for his acuity, but she remained silent. He got out and searched the front of the car for the hood release. His perplexity was obvious, and Stephanie reached in under the dashboard and pulled the release lever. One eyebrow of his twitched as he raised the hood.

"Get on in," he said. She did so, and he said, "When I say now, try the starter."

He reached in and did something to the engine, and then shouted, "Now!"

Stephanie turned the starter over, once, twice, and it seemed to almost catch. But then, no luck. He urged her to keep on. Finally he backed up and slammed the hood down, and then made a motion as if dusting off his hands. He walked around to the other side of the car and looked underneath. Then he came back to Stephanie's side.

"I see what's wrong," he said. "It's the spark."

He imparted this information to Stephanie in the same manner that Churchill addressed the British nation on the eve of the Second World War. She was hoping he would add useful information as to how to solve the crisis he had just identified, but he left his remark about the spark to be carved in stone.

"What must I do, then?" she asked. "Can you fix it?"

Instead of answering, he scratched his head and cocked one eyebrow at Stephanie. "What's your name?" he asked.

"Stephanie. Stephanie Gray," she replied. "But look here, it's getting late, and I need to get my car started." She looked in the car window to see her Indian paintbrushes lying on the seat. They were almost wilted in the heat.

Jerry began to walk away without another word, toward his house. Reluctantly Stephanie followed.

He turned his head slightly to make sure she was coming. "Them flowers are gonna die," he observed.

"They will if you don't help me get home soon," she said. As they neared the porch, she spied an old truck in the yard on the far side of the house.

"Will you take me to town in your truck? I'll pay you for your trouble."

He turned toward her, and she saw a grin start to invade his face. "How much will I get for it?" he asked.

"Well, I don't have a lot of cash, but . . ."

His face fell a little. "No, I'm afraid my truck won't run. I guess you'll have to walk."

Stephanie suddenly remembered the man at the service station. Max. She had his number in her purse.

"May I use your telephone, then?" She remembered leaving her cell phone at home.

"Want to come in a minute?" he said, ignoring her question. He wasn't smiling but his mouth was twisted up in a grin.

"Well, I really would like to use your telephone, if you don't mind."

He had gone into the house, and he held the door open for her. The door had a spring nailed to it to pull it shut. In the center of the room was a large table, which had once been used for a dining table, many years ago. Canned food was sitting on the table, many cans, some of them opened and some still sealed. None had labels on them. The room was evidently the largest of the house, and the odor was oppressive. The older man was nowhere to be seen.

Glancing around, Stephanie saw that there were bed sheets hung at the windows to serve as curtains. To the left at the back of the room a doorway led into a kitchen, and two doors to the right were closed.

Jerry noticed Stephanie's glance at the closed door. "That's my bedroom," he volunteered in a whisper. "Come on and I'll show you."

Stephanie's head reeled. She felt as if she were in a nightmare. "Oh, no," she gasped. "I just want to use the telephone."

"Ain't got one," he said, between his teeth. "You'll have to use the one at the store."

"What store?"

"The store over yonder," he said, gesturing in the general direction of the road on which she had been traveling.

He had his hands on the table, and was edging around it. Stephanie could see that he wanted to put himself between her and the door. His eyes were fixed on her, like a snake stalking a bird. Just as he made a sudden move around the corner of the table, she lunged for the front door and opened it, stepping out onto the porch. She caught sight of the burning light bulb as she hastily stepped off the porch. Then she glanced back. Jerry was hanging back from the light of day, and was framed in the doorway with a leer on his face. She felt she had to say something.

"Thank you, Mr. . ."

"Osgood. Jerry Osgood. You call me Jerry."

"Thank you, Mr. Osgood." But she thought: thanks for nothing.

She walked to the store he had indicated. It wasn't visible from the shack, but it was nestled behind a stand of trees about a mile down the road, in a wooded area bordering the fields.

When she entered the store a little bell rang above the door. Stephanie looked around at the merchandise. It was a store for the farm community all right. Side by side with canned goods there were assorted seeds in large round containers, various items of hardware, and compounds for weed and insect control.

Soon a man came in from the back of the store, wiping his hands on his leather apron. "Hello, miss," he said pleasantly. "Is there anything I can get for you?"

"Yes," replied Stephanie. "I'm new around here, and I've had a little trouble with my car. I left my cell phone at home." Still shaken from the incident at Jerry Osgood's, she bit her lip and tried to hide her nervousness.

She had taken out the slip of paper with the telephone number and the name "Max" written across it in a bold hand. The man showed her the telephone beside the cash register, and she noted a sympathetic look of concern on his face. Inadvertently she dropped the slip of paper.

The man stooped to pick it up for her and glanced at it. "Max," he said. "That can only be one person around here. Max Lamartine."

He handed the slip of paper back to Stephanie. "But you won't need to call him on the telephone," he went on. "He just lives right here."

He walked over to the window to show Stephanie a large house, partly concealed by trees, just down the road a few yards.

As she approached the house she realized it was much larger than it had appeared at first glance. It was a huge antebellum style house, rather forbidding, with a grand brick entranceway and a curving drive leading up to the front and then meandering around to the porte-cochere at the side. But Stephanie stopped dead in her tracks when she saw the name neatly wrought in metal letters on the mailbox: Carmichael.

The day is definitely not going well, thought Stephanie, taking a deep breath as she rang the doorbell.

A pleasant woman answered. "I beg your pardon," said Stephanie, "My car has broken down, and I wondered if there was someone here . . ."

"Come in, child," the woman interrupted. "You look exhausted. Just sit here and I'll go find Mr. Max." She indicated a small bench in the entrance hall, and turned to go into the other part of the house.

What a confusing afternoon, thought Stephanie, left alone in the silent house. Just when she was feeling so good about everything, her car had to act up, throwing her into an unpleasant confrontation with the Osgoods, father and son—if that wretched old man was Jerry Osgood's father. Neither of them had given her any help at all. Now she was sitting here in this magnificent house, waiting for the dark and frightening man named Max. But what about the name on the mailbox?

"So your car has stalled again, pretty one." She hadn't seen him come up, but as she glanced up at his face she felt that same electricity she had sensed at the service station.

"Will you have a cup of coffee, or tea?" he asked. "Something to help calm your nerves."

"Yes, tea, please." She was grateful for his understanding, and she realized she must look very distraught.

"Come in here," he said, leading the way into the next room through a wide double door. It was an elegant dining room, and Stephanie noticed a huge crystal chandelier over the long oak dining table. In no time at all Max had arranged to have tea brought and poured, and Stephanie felt her confidence returning with each sip of the hot liquid.

"I certainly appreciate your kindness," Stephanie said. "But I don't know exactly who you are. The man at the store said you were called Max Lamartine."

"Maximilian Lamartine, at your service," he said, rising and bowing slightly. "But I'm afraid I don't have the pleasure." His eyes were searching hers, and something in his manner made her feel as if he thought her the most important person in the world.

"Oh. Well, my name is Stephanie Gray. I'm Mrs. Eleanor Kimball's granddaughter. Do you know her?"

"I haven't been here very long. But yes, I have heard her name. Now tell me what happened to your car."

Stephanie told him how she had stopped on the highway and about the incident at the Osgood shack, omitting the insinuations Jerry Osgood had flung at her. She simply said that Jerry Osgood hadn't been able to do anything about her car, but that he had said the spark was at fault.

Max smiled at this information. "He's probably right. It's either the spark, or, more likely, the car is very jealous of your beauty."

Stephanie felt the tingle of a blush. She quickly looked at his eyes. They had a twinkle in them and she knew he was having a private joke at her expense. He hadn't taken the remark about the spark seriously at all.

"Well, if it isn't the spark, then what do you think it is, Mr. Lamartine?" she said in a slightly haughty tone.

"I suppose we'll have to go over and find out," he returned. "But by all means, let's drive down in my car. And please call me Max."

He led the way out the side door to his long, opulent black car, standing under the roof of the porte-cochere. He held the door for her, touching her arm, and as she slid into the seat, sinking into the luxurious upholstery, she could feel his eyes on her studying her profile.

Driving out the driveway, the sight of the mailbox brought back the name Carmichael to her. Somehow Maximilian Lamartine must be connected to Irwin Carmichael. She was afraid to ask, afraid to find out the truth. The memories of the anguished look on her grandmother's face telling her about Irwin Carmichael came back to her. She looked over at her companion. He had a curl to his lips, a sensuous expression. Could it be cruel as well? She could see him standing in front of a modest little house, hands on his hips, laughing as he turned a family out of its home, just as she could visualize Irwin Carmichael in the same role.

She looked at him again. He had often been in her thoughts since that first encounter, and in her thoughts he had appeared handsomer than he actually was. She compared him to Jeff Kern. When she had known Jeff years before, he had been a little pudgy, but now he was all muscle and devastatingly handsome. On the other hand, Max Lamartine had a certain nobility about his features, and his eyes gave her the impression of an eagle, searching the horizon. His face was not boyish, like Jeff's, but what she thought of as craggy, with a striking individuality.

"Do you find my profile interesting?" he broke in on her thoughts. She hadn't meant to be so obvious.

"No! I mean, yes! I mean . . . well, you certainly are smooth shaven by contrast with Mr. Osgood." She was caught by surprise, and managed to keep from appearing too flustered.

They pulled up to her car. In a matter of minutes, the engine was purring softly as if it had never stalled.

"Drive over to my house," said Max. "We'll have to get it fixed up, or you might not even get home. How far away do you live?"

"Oh, it's not far," she said. "But I shouldn't have any more trouble. Thanks anyway."

"Who is the mechanic around here, you or me?" he said, and Stephanie could see he was serious. "Follow me. You won't make it if you don't let me do something about the car."

She seemed to have no choice. As they arrived at his house, she glanced over at the flowers on the seat beside her. They looked wilted and dead.

"Let me see the flowers," said Max, standing at the side of the car. "It shouldn't take them a minute to spruce up in a little water."

He took the Indian paintbrushes into the house and gave them to the care of Mrs. Roberts, the housekeeper who had first met Stephanie at the door. She snipped the ends and put them in water. Stephanie was left to watch the operation while Max absented himself for a few minutes.

Mrs. Roberts was the epitome of the housekeeper for a large country place. Her iron-gray hair was severely pulled back in a bun, more for convenience than appearance. As she spoke her lips gave the impression of matter-of-factness. "You can see they are already beginning to appreciate the drink," she said of the flowers, narrowing her eyes in appraisal.

"Oh, they don't really matter," put in Stephanie. "I just picked them by the side of the road."

"Nonsense. They're as pretty as can be. A group like this should be on a dinner table."

Max came in at that moment, forestalling Stephanie's reply. He said that Jake was taking care of the car, but that Stephanie would have to stay for another hour or so while he worked on it. She glanced at her watch. It was after five, and her grandmother would be worrying if she didn't show up for dinner.

"I wonder if I might use your telephone, then," she said. "I'll have to call my grandmother to let her know I won't be there for dinner. She might worry."

"By all means." Max showed the way to a little alcove which contained a telephone stand and seat. "Tell her you are staying to dinner with me."

"But I can't . . . I don't want to intrude. Besides that, I don't even know you."

"What better way to get acquainted than over dinner. You don't have much choice anyway, do you? I promise the dinner will be very tasty. No arguments, now."

When her grandmother answered, Stephanie promised to tell her about her entire day when she got in if it wasn't too late, and said that she shouldn't worry because everything was fine.

When she finished on the telephone, she went into the sitting room adjoining the large dining room in which she had taken tea. There she found Max Lamartine seated at a very elegant roll-top desk, which was literally covered with papers of various sorts. The computer was idle, but Max was poring over one of the legal-sized sheaves of paper, and didn't notice her entrance.

Stephanie gave a little cough to announce her presence. "Hard at work, I see," she said.

She had surprised him, and he looked up. "Yes," he replied, pushing his chair back. I'm trying to make heads or tails of a very sticky situation. But please," he continued, rising, "I'm forgetting my manners. Take a seat." He indicated a wing-back chair beside a low side table of mahogany.

"It looks as if you're in the midst of some important business. Don't let me interrupt."

"Not an interruption at all," he replied. "It's nothing important—I can take care of this any time." He clipped the papers before him together and laid them in a prominent spot among the other papers on the desk. Then he rose and walked to a small sideboard near the door.

"Will you have a dry sherry before dinner?"

"Thank you."

He took a seat near her and glanced at her with his piercing eyes. "You aren't from this area, are you? What brings you to the Delta? Don't tell me. Let me take a guess. You are a reporter for a glamorous New York magazine, and you are here to do an article on the depressed living conditions in the Delta. Am I right?"

Stephanie laughed. "No, you're entirely wrong. In the first place, I'm not a reporter. Besides that, living conditions aren't so depressed here. And what makes you so sure I'm not from this area?"

"Oh, just call it intuition. Or better yet, put it down to my amazing ability to recognize subtle differences in speech inflection. Think of me as an

American Professor Higgins." He chuckled. "Seriously, what does bring you here?"

"I admit it, Professor. I'm from St. Louis— lived there most of my life, except for a year or two here as a teenager. I worked at Chariton Products— in St. Louis—for a couple of years. My father and I were very close, and when he died, I just felt—well, at loose ends. Besides that, my grandmother is getting on in years, and she wanted me to come stay with her." For some reason Stephanie felt drawn to tell Max even the most personal things about herself. He seemed to kindle her confidence.

"Is she Judson Kimball's wife?"

"Well, she's his widow. But how did you know? Oh, I suppose everyone around here knew my grandfather."

"Yes, perhaps they did." He gave an inadvertent glance to the papers on the desk. "But now I think dinner is about ready," he said, taking a sign from Mrs. Roberts in the doorway.

"I hope you don't think my questions were rude," he said, as they went into the dining room. "But I have one more. Did you do a lot of office work at Chariton Products?"

Stephanie was a little surprised by the question, but she was pleased with her employment record, and was quick to answer.

"Yes, as a matter of fact. We had a Dell PC, and I did a lot of typing—dictation, letters, memos, bookkeeping, charts, work hours—also filing and operation of various office machines. Not a large company. I was an executive secretary, and often acted as receptionist for an office of . . . but you don't want to know all that," she said with a little laugh. "To answer your question, yes, I did a lot of office work."

Max laughed with her. "Whew! Enough, enough! I can tell you're highly qualified.

The dinner was set for two under the chandelier. Mrs. Roberts had put a vase with the colorful flowers—now fully revived—on the table. Stephanie found to her surprise that she was hungry, and the veal was delicious.

Max said he lived in Memphis, where he was involved in business. He didn't venture to say what sort of business, so Stephanie, emboldened by the light rosé that accompanied the meal, asked.

"Well, in fact, it's a textile plant. We manufacture cotton goods, linens, and other cloths, along with our various lines of clothing. Interestingly enough, we process much of the cotton that is grown right here in the Delta. All of which has nothing to do with why I'm here."

The name Carmichael suddenly stabbed through Stephanie's thoughts. With an effort to moderate her voice, she said, "What is it about Carmichael? I saw the name on the mailbox." In spite of her self control, she blurted the name out and managed to sound as if she were accusing Max of murdering helpless infants.

He appeared nonchalant. "Ah, yes, of course. Irwin Carmichael. Uncle Irwin. I suppose everyone around here has come into contact with Uncle Irwin sometime or another. He died last year, and I'm his only heir."

Stephanie rose from her place. She had finished dinner, and she was exerting an effort to be polite. "I thank you for your kindness, and for the dinner," she said stiffly. "Is my car running?"

Mrs. Roberts had gone out, and she now returned with Jake, Max's helper and handyman. "The car shouldn't be giving you any more trouble, miss," he said.

"Was it the spark?" she asked.

"Spark?" said Jake. "No'm, it was just a problem with the fuel pump."

Stephanie walked to the door almost in a trance. Did Maximilian Lamartine know what kind of man his uncle was, and did he care? Again the image of Max came to her thoughts, and she could now see Irwin Carmichael standing with him, with his arm on his shoulder. The family was being ejected, and their eyes were turned up as in supplication. But a devilish grin was on the faces of Carmichael and his nephew.

"Let me get your flowers," said Mrs. Roberts, as Stephanie stepped into her car.

"No," said Stephanie. "You're very kind. But you keep them for the table." Then she thought: *You may need them to brighten your life before long.*

Perhaps Max didn't know. As she drove off, she could see him standing in the doorway with an innocent and puzzled look on his face, as if he actually didn't know how much heartache his uncle had caused, as if he didn't know he was now reaping the benefits from the ill-gotten gains Irwin Carmichael had acquired by a lifetime of grinding people's lives under his heel.

Four

Friends

When Stephanie got back home it was after eight o'clock. Mrs. Kimball was pleased and relieved to see her, even though she tried not to let Stephanie know she had been anxious.

"I'm glad you called to let me know you would be late. You will have to tell me about your car. But first, did you have enough dinner? You didn't say where you were planning to eat."

Stephanie didn't know whether her grandmother knew who Max was—that he was a Carmichael—but she figured it would come out sooner or later. She took a deep breath.

"I had dinner with a very kind man named Max Lamartine. Do you know him?" She shot her grandmother a quick glance.

"Lamartine. No the name is not familiar to me. He must be new to the area. But then, I've been a little out of touch lately—I don't know everyone around here. How was your dinner with Mr. Lamartine?"

"It was delicious. We had . . . well, we had a very nice meal and Mr. Lamartine had my car repaired. It runs like a top now. I want to tell you about Nola, too, and Jeff, but right now, Grandmother, I've had a rough day and I think I need to go to bed early."

Stephanie was grateful for the comfort of the bed, and as her head hit the pillow she knew she would drop off to sleep immediately.

But she couldn't sleep. She tossed and turned and thought about Nola and Jeff, and about the luncheon, and the dinner at the home of Max Lamartine, and Mrs. Roberts, and the Indian paintbrushes. She thought about the unsavory incident with Jerry Osgood.

But her mind kept returning to Maximilian Lamartine. For all his seeming kindness she knew him to be a despicable creature, carrying on in the tradition his uncle had established—bleeding his neighbors dry, ruining the hopes and dreams and lives of everyone who was unfortunate enough to be associated in any way with him.

Tired as she was, Stephanie found it impossible to sleep. So she went down to the kitchen to get a glass of milk in hopes that it would help her drop off. The night light was on in the kitchen, and she sat at the table with her glass.

She was fifteen again. She had come down for a midnight snack, and there sat her grandfather with his head in his hands and papers spread out all over the kitchen table.

He looked so distressed Stephanie came up and put her arms around his neck. "Did you come down for a midnight snack too, Grampa?"

"No . . . well, yes I did. Sit down there, and let's have a little something together."

Stephanie knew her grandfather had to drink milk frequently, because of his stomach condition. And lately he had not been getting enough sleep—it was evident that something was bothering him.

"What are all these papers, Grampa?"

"Oh child, these are just some business papers. I don't think you would understand."

"Try me. I might even be able to help." She didn't have the slightest idea how she could help, but she spoke with confidence.

"Now you know you ought to go back to bed. It's too late for a pretty little thing like you to be up."

"Oh, please, Grampa." She gave him another little squeeze.

"Well, all right. Bring your chair over. But you have to promise me not to tell your grandmother about this—I don't want her to worry."

They talked about the land mortgages, and the pasture lands for his few milk cows, and the prices he got for his cotton and beans and other crops, and about the cost of maintaining his equipment, and about the salaries he had to pay the hands.

"Who determines the prices you get for your crops, Grampa?"

"Ultimately we do, by the prices we pay at the store for dry goods and food. And the crops go through a sort of auction bid process—pretty complicated. But if the system is going to work— and it does work—each person or business along the line has to make a little profit. Don't you see, the grocer, the packer, the processor, the buyer, and the farmer—all make a little from the price the consumer pays. It's like the farmer is the first link in a long chain. But because he is the first link, he doesn't have much control over how much profit he can make in any year."

"Then it seems that the person who buys your harvest is able to juggle it around and make all the profit he wants."

"Not quite, child, because of various regulations, and the watchful eye of the Grange. Another thing that keeps the buyer from making all the profit is competition. You see, if I were able to sell to any one of several buyers, I would probably get a very fair price. And to a certain extent, I can. But the trouble is, because of many other factors that don't seem to have much to do with the situation, like the weather, for example, I have to sell most of what I produce to one man who controls all the links in the chain all the way down the line. So he is able to manipulate the market and the profits to his own advantage. And when he does that someone has to take a loss." He looked at Stephanie. "Guess who it is that takes a loss."

"Oh, Grampa, that doesn't seem fair."

"It's not fair, Stephanie. It's mostly illegal, too. But nobody can seem to prove anything against Mr. Carmichael. One thing, he is not only the main buyer for my crops, he also owns or controls most of the other business interests in the area. For example, if I want a loan from the bank, he can fix it so I won't get the loan."

"How can he do that, Grampa? I know Mr. Griggs at the bank. He would be fair to you, wouldn't he?"

"Sure, he would if he could. But it's a little more complicated than that. Even though it's not quite . . . well not quite legal, I guess . . . still, Mr. Carmichael has a hold over Mr. Griggs. A sort of personal hold. He can put the squeeze on Mr. Griggs if he wants to. And consequently, Mr. Griggs had to do just about whatever Mr. Carmichael wants him to. Do you understand that?"

"I suppose I do. Then Mr. Carmichael—he's our enemy, isn't he?"

"I wouldn't put it quite like that, Stephanie. I still have to do business with him, and for the most part things work out all right. It's just that . . . well, he has me in pretty much of a bind right now." The old man brought his clenched fist noiselessly down on the stack of papers in frustration.

Stephanie looked at her grandfather in alarm. His veins stood out on his temples. Her heart went out to him, and she knew that even though she had volunteered, she couldn't do anything to help him. Nobody could.

"Pour me just a little more milk, will you, girl? I think I'm going on back to bed."

They had both returned to their beds. The memory was still vivid in Stephanie's mind as she sat there with her milk in the half dark kitchen. She had thought things would be better for her grandfather the next morning, but they weren't. She didn't have any more discussions about Mr. Carmichael's tyranny with him, but she could see over the next few months that he was still under a heavy burden. She spent her birthday with her grandparents in August, and then, despite the pain of parting from the friends she had made in school during the past year and a half, it was back St. Louis for her. Less than two years later, her grandfather was dead.

"He's at peace now, she thought, as she set her glass on the counter. And I suppose Grandmother was at least partially right about Irwin Carmichael, hounding my grandfather to death. She realized that all the bitterness she had against Irwin Carmichael was now centered on his nephew, Maximilian Lamartine. How arrogant he seemed.

Several days passed without event, during which Stephanie helped her grandmother do some canning. With Betsy, she picked some of the last peaches of the season from the trees in the orchard. She found the country life to be an exhilarating change from her existence in St. Louis.

She was just washing her hands from the peaches when Betsy answered the telephone. "It's for you, Stephanie," she said. "I think he said his name was Marv."

What an annoyance, thought Stephanie. She certainly didn't want Marv Woods' attention, knowing about the volatile situation between him and Janie. Janie already disliked and distrusted her, and she was afraid it would only get worse and lead to strained relations between her and Nola.

She picked up the receiver, wondering what she could tell Marv.

"Hello."

"Hello, Stephanie. This is Marv Woods. Remember we met the other day with Nola and Jeff."

"Yes, of course I remember." She wasn't sure whether to be cool or friendly.

"I hope you're getting accustomed to country life by now. It isn't as bad as some would have you believe." He was obviously referring to Janie's remarks.

"I like it fine," she replied. "Don't forget I lived here nearly two years."

"Yes," he said. He was silent for a moment, and Stephanie could sense that he was screwing up his courage.

"Stephanie, they are having an old-fashioned barn dance at Miller's Place this Saturday, and I wonder if you would like to go with me. It should be lots of fun."

"But I thought you and Janie . . ."

"No, Janie and I aren't—steady, or engaged, or anything like that. We just see one another once in a while, that's all. Besides that, she's gone out of town for a while. You will go, won't you?"

Oh, why not, she thought. "If you're sure I won't be cutting in on something," she said. "What about Nola and Jeff? Will they be there?"

"Sure they will. We can make it a sort of foursome. Maybe we can stop at the Donut Hole afterward for a snack."

Marv picked her up in his neat blue car early on Saturday. Miller's Place had been built as a barn—a huge one—but now it was fixed up for public meetings, dances, auctions, and even roller skating.

Stephanie was a little surprised at the huge crowd at Miller's. She hadn't thought there were that many people in all of Stanley. She glanced around the large hall and noted the many tables with two, four, and six couples at them. And all along the two long sides of the building people were sitting and standing, sometimes clustered in knots, sometimes watching the rest of the crowd wistfully as if hoping for a friendly glance. She and Marv found an empty table, and as he seated her she saw that people were still pouring in the door.

Nola and Jeff appeared, edging their way toward the table Marv and Stephanie had taken. They were seated near the side door and as Nola sat beside Stephanie they exchanged a friendly greeting. Stephanie commented on the large crowd.

"This is an annual event, sponsored by the local Grange," Nola explained. "It's an old custom around here to have a get-together celebrating the end of the harvest season. Last year it was loads of fun." Her blue eyes cut around to Jeff, and Stephanie could sense something pass between the two.

"It was our first date," whispered Jeff with a little smile.

Stephanie was happy for her friends and slightly envious at the same time. She looked at Marv out of the corner of her eye. He was certainly attracted to her. And he was quite a handsome man. Suddenly the image of Max loomed before her eyes, and she mentally compared the two men. Max possessed a certain individuality—that she couldn't deny. He wasn't the male model type that Jeff and Marv seemed to be, except that he had that rugged, dark look one sometimes saw in television ads.

Then the realization that she was daydreaming, daydreaming about Max, came to her. A dance was starting, and Marv tapped her on the shoulder.

"Would you do me the honor?" Marv asked.

Marv was a good dancer, and Stephanie realized that she hadn't been on a dance floor in at least a year. She thoroughly enjoyed it, even though Marv kept trying to hold her closer and closer. She certainly didn't want to lead him on.

As the evening wore on, Stephanie enjoyed herself more and more. Both Marv and Jeff were good dancers. Marv appeared to be getting a little tipsy, but he was only comic rather than obnoxious. Nola told Stephanie quite a lot about her plans for the future.

Stephanie decided to ask Nola if she knew anything about Max. It couldn't help his image in Stephanie's eyes, but she felt the need to have that image confirmed. She waited till Jeff and Marv were both away from the table, and then leaned over to Nola.

"Nola, I hesitated to tell you about this before, but now I want to get it off my chest. The day we had lunch together, my car broke down on the road, and I had the most horrid experience. I went and knocked on the door of a little house by the side of the road for help. A man answered—a man named Jerry Osgood."

Nola raised her eyes in a gesture of irritation. "Everybody knows about Jerry Osgood," she said. "He's really a low-life tramp, he and his father both. Some people feel sorry for him, but I don't think he deserves anybody's pity. What did he do?"

"He looked at my car, but he couldn't do anything to make it run. He really didn't help me at all. But he did get rather fresh with me."

"Did you go into his house?"

"Yes, it was . . . well, very untidy."

"I'll bet it was! Untidy to say the least. I'm surprised he didn't try to force you into his bedroom."

"He made some very suggestive remarks, but I left as quickly as I could." She didn't want to go into the way he had tried to pin her away from the front door.

Nola looked around the large room. "I saw him here a while ago."

"Really! I can't imagine him coming to a dance like this. It seems too—too nice."

"You may rest assured he didn't come here for the same reasons we did. He's probably got his eye on somebody and came here to try his luck with her. But you didn't say how you got your car running."

"I finally got help from a man named Lamartine." Stephanie searched her friend's face for a sign of recognition.

"Max Lamartine. Of course he would help. He's only been here a couple of months. I understand he's busy with the estate left by Irwin Carmichael . . ." She gave her friend an inquisitive look. "I don't know if you know about Irwin Carmichael."

"I . . . well, I have heard various things from my grandparents."

"He was undoubtedly the wealthiest man around here. He spent most of his life acquiring riches, and he died recently. Just between you and me, most of the people around here weren't sorry to see him go. His assets and real estate underwent a probate, and now it appears this man named Max Lamartine is his only heir. I don't know if his estate is even settled yet.

"By the way," she continued, "your Max Lamartine is probably here tonight."

Stephanie glanced around the room, but she couldn't see much because of the throng of dancers.

"I've only seen him one time," said Nola. "Tell me about him. What's he like?"

Stephanie was almost afraid to tell Nola what her feelings about Max were. For one thing, she wasn't sure how she felt about him herself. Besides, she couldn't quite tell from Nola's remarks how Nola felt about Irwin Carmichael. She found herself speaking all too glowingly about Max.

"He was very kind to me. After my trying afternoon—and it <u>was</u> trying—he fixed up my car and gave me a delicious dinner. He was very considerate."

"He sounds very nice. Tell me more."

"Well, there's not a lot to tell." Against her will Stephanie gave an unconscious sigh. "I said he was kind and considerate. But that's not all. He made me feel right at home in his house, and I could almost imagine myself—" She broke off. She nearly said '—in his arms.' "I could almost imagine myself living in a place like that."

"I suppose he lives in Carmichael's old house?"

Stephanie nodded. Nola was perceptive, and Stephanie saw a gleam come into her eyes. She suddenly became serious.

"Don't tell me you're falling for Max Lamartine. Because if you are, I have something to tell you about him."

Here it comes, thought Stephanie. But suddenly Jeff and Marv were standing beside the table, asking for a dance.

Stephanie was too lost in her thoughts to talk during the dance, even though Marv kept trying to draw her out with innumerable questions. As they left the dance floor, she suddenly felt a little nauseous from all the excitement and bustle. She excused herself from the table, ignoring Marv's solicitous queries, and headed for the side door.

Stephanie stepped out into the moonlit night and was immediately transported into another world. Here and there patches of shadow from oleander bushes dotted the gentle slope of the lawn, and on Stephanie's left, toward the back of the building, she could see a low magnolia tree with its fragrant white blossoms, guarding the approach to the tangle of woods that surrounded the building on three sides. She was braced by the whole outdoor aspect, and the fresh air made her feel better immediately.

She walked over to the magnolia tree and put out a hand to touch one of the blossoms. The underside of the blossom felt smooth and cool to her touch, and the heady fragrance pervaded her senses. All of a sudden she felt a rough hand grasping her arm. She jerked her hand around and saw a masculine form in the shadow.

"Oh," she exclaimed. She couldn't see who it was, and Max's image sprang to her mind. Instinctively she backed away, but he still had her arm in his firm grip. As he came into the moonlight from the shadows, she saw his face: it was Jerry Osgood.

"Out for a little moonlight walk, eh?"

"Well, yes, if it's any of your business."

She tried to collect her thoughts. If she screamed, she wouldn't be heard above the band and the noise of the crowd inside. She tried to wrench her arm from his grip.

"Not so fast," he said. "I'm not letting you go this easy. Ever since you came to my house that day, I've been waiting for the chance to get you alone. Come on with me and don't make any fuss." He pulled her into the shadows of the woodsy path.

"Let me go!" she cried.

"Not till I've had a look at you." With his free hand he pulled at her blouse, ripping it off one shoulder and exposing her bare flesh.

Stephanie gave a little scream of mortification.

"Now that's what I call . . ." he began. But someone jerked him around, away from Stephanie, and landed a stunning blow on his jaw.

"Let her go, you beast." It was Max.

"You're just jealous," howled Jerry, holding his jaw. He evidently knew better than to try his strength against Max. He lunged again at Stephanie and pinned her arms, wrapping his hands around her from behind.

"You're too late," he flung at Max. "I have a claim on this tidbit. I saw her first. Just leave us alone."

Max was astonished by Jerry's brash action. He looked at Stephanie, pinned in Jerry's arms, but the darkness prevented him from seeing her face. She was sobbing and choking, and with an effort she pulled free from Jerry and ran into Max's arms.

"Oh, Max, please help me." She covered her face in fear and shame.

Jerry was persistent. Half crazed with lust and wrought into an excited fever by the blow he had taken on the chin, he grabbed Max's arm and tried to pull Stephanie away, yelling curses at Max.

Max slightly released his hold on Stephanie, and landed another fist on Jerry's face, this time sending him sprawling to the ground.

"I'm warning you, Jerry Osgood, and this is the only warning you'll get from me," said Max in a menacing tone. "Stay away from this girl. You'll end up in the hospital next time."

Jerry was sitting on the ground in a daze. He was panting heavily. "All right, Mr. Smart Man," he whined. "You can have her this time, but just you wait."

Jerry slunk off into the darkness of the woods, and Max took Stephanie tenderly into his arms. He helped her over to a low bench beside the building. She leaned her head on his chest and felt her strength returning, as if borrowing from his own vitality.

She had straightened out her torn blouse as best she could. After a few minutes she found her voice. "It looks like you are always helping me," she said. "But how did you happen to be out here? I didn't see you at the dance."

"I was there, all right. I just caught a glimpse of you as you went out the door alone. Then I saw Osgood following you, and as soon as I could excuse myself from the people I was with, I came out. I had an idea Jerry was up to no good." Max was looking away from Stephanie, and she could see his chiseled features silhouetted by the light from the building.

"Never mind about Osgood now," he went on. "I have a feeling your friends will be getting anxious about you. What do you want to do about them?"

She raised her head from his chest. Here she was, her heart almost torn in two by the feeling of security and safety in his arms against the fact that he was, after all, Maximilian Lamartine, of the Carmichael clan.

"In your condition I think you shouldn't go back into the dance," he was saying. Her blouse was badly ripped, hanging tattered from her shoulder. "Here come your friends looking for you."

She looked up to see Jeff and Nola peering out into the darkness. They saw her and came over.

"We missed you," said Nola. Stephanie rose, feeling her legs weak under her.

"We wondered if you were all right," said Jeff. "At first I thought you were dancing, but when you didn't come back to the table, we got a little worried."

They weren't able to see the condition of Stephanie's disarray in the shadow of the building, but Nola sensed something was amiss.

"Oh, Nola, I've had a terrible experience." Stephanie bit her lip and held onto Jeff's proffered hand. She briefly told them that Jerry Osgood had attacked her in the dark, omitting most of the unpleasant details. Max had risen and she turned to include him in the circle. Jeff looked at him with a slightly puzzled expression.

"This is Max Lamartine," said Stephanie. "He has come to my aid again, and I feel I'll never be out of his debt."

The couple shook hands with Max. Nola gave him a pleasant smile. "Mr. Lamartine?" she said. "We've heard a great deal about you in Stanley. Will you be here long?"

"My business won't allow me to stay long enough, I'm afraid," replied Max. "I'm quite charmed by the friendliness of the people here."

"Thank you," said Nola, on behalf of the city of Stanley. "Oh, but did you . . . are you here at the dance alone?"

"Yes, quite alone. Actually, Mr. and Mrs. Springer took it upon themselves to amuse me for the evening, but they are quite immersed in their circle of friends."

Stephanie peered toward the door. "I don't see Marv," she said to Jeff. "He didn't come out with you?"

"No, he was dancing," replied Jeff. "I don't think he's even aware of our absence. But maybe I should go fetch him." He moved toward the open door.

"No, Jeff, don't," said Stephanie, catching his arm. "I just couldn't go back in, not with the condition my clothes are in." Jeff saw for the first time how badly torn her blouse was.

"I'll be glad to give you a lift home," put in Max. My car is just out front."

Stephanie resisted the sudden urge to lean against Max's chest, to feel again the security of his arms around her. Then she heard herself saying, "Well, if it's not too much trouble. Jeff and Nola can tell Marv that I had a friend take me home. They can explain without going into too much detail." As she talked to Max, she was aware of the strange sensation that he and she were alone in the universe, talking together, oblivious of everything else.

Jeff's voice intruded upon the current that seemed to be passing between her and Max: "Marv will be glad, actually, not to have his evening interrupted. He's become occupied with some . . . friends." Jeff gave a wry smile with the corner of his mouth. He turned to Max. "It's good of you to look after Stephanie," he said in a fatherly way, shaking Max's hand warmly. Stephanie was amused at his manner, for he was at least five years Max's junior.

Arm in arm Nola and Stephanie walked toward the door of the building. "I'll call tomorrow," promised Nola. "I want you to count on me as a friend." She kissed Stephanie lightly on the cheek.

"Thanks," said Stephanie. "I needed that. I'm sorry to have ruined your evening, though."

"Nonsense," said Nola. "It's not any trouble for us. Maybe we can have an evening together sometime soon, though. Are you sure you won't need me and Jeff?"

"Thanks, no. Mr. Lamartine will see me home."

Stephanie skooched down into the cushion of the dark upholstery in Max's huge car as he pulled out of the lot.

"I've been quite a bother for you," she said. "Now your friends will miss you at the dance."

He remained silent.

"By the way," continued Stephanie in a teasing manner, "I didn't see you on the dance floor. Don't you like these provincial dances?"

"On the contrary,' he replied, "I did dance one set with Mrs. Springer." Stephanie shot him a quizzical glance. "She's Bill Springer's wife—he's the Director of the First Bank of Stanley."

"Oh." Stephanie sank further back into the cushions.

"There was only one girl there who took my fancy," he continued. "I didn't get a chance to dance with her."

Stephanie's breath came quicker. She was beginning to feel miffed, but her reason told her she had no cause to feel so. His attitude, however, was beginning to seem intolerable. He obviously looks down his nose at everything and everybody in Stanley, except the bank VIP, she mused. Then he picks and chooses among the local girls for the prettiest one to fix his attentions on. Well, in that case she was glad he had become occupied with her difficulty with that worm, Jerry Osgood. It kept him from imposing himself on some innocent girl.

She looked over at him. His black eyes reflected the headlights of the car, and his features in profile reminded her of a Caesar. His mouth was curled in the hint of a disdainful smile.

"Humph," she mumbled. "Only one girl you fancied? She was probably Stanley's prettiest—the belle of the ball." Her voice carried a slight hint of sarcasm.

"I should say she was the belle of the ball," he confirmed. He glanced at Stephanie in her corner. "She was preoccupied most of the time, even when Jerry Osgood followed her out the door."

"Oh, Max," she said involuntarily, reaching a hand up to her blouse. The incident was too recent for her not to feel shame. She was glad the darkness concealed her pink flush.

"No matter," he said, reading her thoughts. "It's over, and I don't think you'll have to worry about him again."

The incident of the last hour crowded in on her thoughts, and she began to feel slightly queasy. "I'm sorry to ask, but would you pull over for a minute? I'm afraid I'm not feeling well."

Max rolled the car onto the wide shoulder. Stephanie closed her eyes and after a short time began to feel better. His hand was on her shoulder and she looked up at his face. Again she felt that inexplicable current between them. She recalled with all her senses the feeling she had experienced when he had held her in his arms to comfort her after that harrowing episode.

It didn't seem like a conscious action on the part of Stephanie or Max, but suddenly they came together, and their lips met. At first it was a gentle kiss, as if Max were simply telling her that he was there, that his strength was to be used, to be relied upon.

She felt his arm encircling her waist, and clung to him as a drowning swimmer clings to a lifeline. She felt his tongue, delicately searching the softness of her lips. As she yielded to him, his lips became more impetuous, searching.

Then she pushed him away. "No, Max, it can't be like this." He was taking advantage of her vulnerability. She had just come through a very trying experience and hadn't the strength and certainly not much will power left to resist him.

But he had come to her rescue, and she was afraid now she had hurt his feelings.

"I'm sorry," she said. "I don't want to be used. It's not anything about you." She squeezed his hand and gave him a little half-smile. "Please take me home, Max."

He started the car. "Well, at least you're calling me by my given name," he said with a touch of flippancy. "May I call you Stephanie, then?"

The humor was a little lost on her, owing to her emotional state. She thought the question was rather inane, in the circumstances, and she told him so. She squeezed his hand again.

"After all, you've just done battle for me within the last half hour, and I considered it the height of gallantry, not to mention ample reason for the familiarity of first names."

It was Max's turn to feel slightly abashed, but he didn't show it. He smiled and looked down at her. Their eyes met. Without thinking she had reached up to stroke his hand, resting on her shoulder. Again she felt that current between them, and she felt a certain tingling sensation, something she had never felt before, not even when she had thought herself in love with Leon Ainsworth.

The thought of Leon made her shudder slightly, and she seemed to come to her senses, pushing Max's hand off her shoulder and sitting up straight in her seat.

Stephanie looked again at Max, whose expression hadn't altered. This was a man for whom she ought to feel only an utter revulsion, but who almost had her under his spell, more than likely the same sort of spell Leon had on her during those months of torture.

I must resist his charm, she thought. I can't let him control me in the way Leon did, and I can't let him take advantage of me like his uncle took advantage of every person he came into contact with. Yet at the same time he has shown me every consideration, he has gone out of his way to help me, and there's no way I know of to repay him. On the other hand he may be simply trying to compromise me. For a moment she thought of offering to pay him for the ride home, but then decided he would consider it an insult.

He pulled the car up to her grandmother's house. Stephanie looked anxiously at the house, hoping her grandmother wouldn't be awake. She would never be able to explain her torn blouse without many embarrassing questions—questions she didn't want to try to answer. And she was half afraid for her grandmother to meet Max, considering he was the spawn of the Carmichaels.

A light was on in the living room. Usually Betsy turned out the lights after bedtime, and Stephanie had expected to find her way in with only the porch light for her key and the hall light inside the door.

Max went round the car to open the door, and she held his arm as they walked up to the house. She knew she should invite him in. Instead, she said nervously, "Everyone's gone to bed, I think. Goodnight, and thank you again."

Stephanie looked out the little side window by the door and saw Max walking back to his car. Just at that moment she heard a voice from the lighted living room cry out in distress: "Stephanie, is that you? Oh, Stephanie, come help me."

It was Betsy. Stephanie stepped quickly over to the open archway and saw her grandmother sprawled out on the floor, with a little trickle of blood running onto the carpet.

"Oh, Grandmother," she cried. "I'll get help." She raced to the door and out onto the porch. Max was just backing his car out, and she thought she was too late. But when he got to the end of the driveway he stopped an instant and then drove back in.

"It's my grandmother, she's been hurt," said Stephanie in as calm a voice as she could muster. Max rushed past her into the living room.

Betsy was standing by Mrs. Kimball, wringing her hands, with tears running down her cheeks.

Mrs. Kimball groaned. "Stephanie, I took a bad fall. It's not as bad as it looks but I did cut my arm on the lamp." The hurricane lamp was on the floor, and the glass globe was shattered. "I can't get up by myself," she continued, "and Betsy isn't able to lift me."

She blinked her eyes and noticed Max for the first time. He bent over to help her up. "We'll soon have you all right again, Mrs. Kimball," he said as he effortlessly lifted her into her wheel chair. "Let me see how badly your arm is cut."

"Grandmother, this is Max Lamartine," said Stephanie. Even in the circumstances, she felt she had to make introductions. Betsy was cleaning up the broken glass.

"Well, young man, you have come just in the nick of time to see me at my worst," said Mrs. Kimball. Max was examining her arm.

"Get me some rubbing alcohol and cotton," he told Betsy. "Also a bandage. I think it's just a surface cut."

"If it is just a surface cut, it sure is a painful one," said Mrs. Kimball. She winced as he cleaned the wound with alcohol. "But I think I'm lucky I didn't break any bones. At my age, you always run a danger of breaking something."

Stephanie had taken advantage of the activity to get a shawl from the hall closet to drape over her torn blouse. "Tell us what happened, Grandmother, if you feel like talking."

With a sure hand, Max was applying a bandage to the cut. Stephanie helped as best she could. "I'll get you something from the kitchen if you like," she offered.

"I think a drop of that brandy I see on the sideboard would be the best thing for your grandmother," said Max.

When Mrs. Kimball had swallowed some of the brandy, she sighed. "That's better. But I suppose you want to know what happened, and why I wasn't in bed long ago. I had decided to wait up, since I was having a little trouble with my asthma. When ten o'clock came and you hadn't appeared, I was too tired to stay up any longer. I tried to get over to my wheel chair without my cane, and stumbled. As I went down, I caught at the lamp table, and we went down together. Betsy came running in, but she couldn't lift me, and just then we heard you come in."

She smiled at Max. "Young man, you have proven to be an angel of mercy to me and to my granddaughter. And this isn't the first time. I'm afraid we'll always be in your debt."

She was breathing hard, and Stephanie noticed that she looked extremely tired. "I think you ought to go to bed now, Grandmother. I suspect you will sleep like a log."

As Mrs. Kimball and Betsy entered the elevator, the older woman looked up at Max. "Young man, I would like to see more of you. Do visit us whenever it's convenient for you." She gave a meaningful glance to Stephanie.

"Thank you. I intend to do just that."

Stephanie walked with Max to the door. "Even in difficult circumstances," he said, your grandmother is charming."

Stephanie was at a loss for words. She had been thanking Max all evening for the way he seemed to always be on hand to rescue her, and she felt her words would be repetitious. She looked up at him, fearing to let her emotions show.

"If only . . . oh, Max, why is it . . ." She broke off. She wanted to cry out to him, to tell him how she felt. But she didn't know how she felt; she only knew the reality of that magnetism that seemed to draw her to him. He was a Carmichael. But even if he weren't a Carmichael, she couldn't tell what it meant—that feeling of electricity between them that was so strong and unmistakable. Did he feel it too?

Her words had trailed off in confusion. She couldn't bring herself to say his name in the same breath with the name Carmichael.

"Why is it?" he echoed. "Why is what?" He obviously could sense the conflict within her, even though she didn't want him to notice how emotionally upset she was.

She knew he would try to kiss her, and she was prepared. She would refuse to kiss him—would put her hand in front of his lips.

Now he was holding her chin in his hand and looking into her eyes. She was lost in the sea of his gaze, keenly aware of the feel of his hand on her face. She knew she couldn't resist him as she had planned.

He turned away. "We can talk more some other time," he said, and was out the door.

Five

Treasure Cove

Two rather uneventful days passed. It was early in the morning when Stephanie was awakened by a light tap at the bedroom door.

"Just a minute," she called. She slipped on a dressing gown and went to the door.

"It's the telephone for you, miss," said Betsy. "I wasn't sure you'd be up, but I asked him to hold."

"Thank you, Betsy." Oh, she thought, if it's Marv Woods I don't know what I'll say. He's due with an apology, the way he ignored me at the dance.

But it wasn't Marv. The deep voice of Max Lamartine greeted her when she answered.

"I hope I didn't wake you too early."

"Oh, no, I was just getting some coffee," she lied.

"I won't keep you. A simple yes or no will do. You see, I just came in to work on these papers—you remember seeing them on the desk— and, well, I could use some help. Someone who is handy on the computer. Someone who can type a clean and neat letter, who can do rather routine office tasks neatly and efficiently—in short, I'm over my ears in this paperwork: deeds, court rulings, and lots of other things that would take me years to wade through by myself. I remembered what a super person you are for those kinds of things, and I want to offer you a job, of sorts."

Stephanie was almost at a loss for words. On the one hand, she wasn't sure she could work with Max every day. His relationship to Irwin Carmichael would be a constant reminder of what he had done to her grandparents. And as Carmichael's nephew, Max was an unknown quantity. Too often she had thought she saw subtle indications of his latent cruelty. More than likely he was following in his uncle's footsteps.

"Well, I'm rather busy right now, but . . ."

"Oh, I'll pay you for your time. And it will only involve half days, say nine till one. If you don't do it, I'll be forced to settle for a less efficient person. Believe me, I'm asking you on your own recommendation.

"Well, I have references, if . . ."

"As if I couldn't trust your word. Of course," he cajoled, "if you feel you're not up to the tasks at hand . . ."

"I certainly am! And the answer is yes. When do you want me to begin?"

"Today. Right now. In fact, how soon can you be here?"

"Hold on. Let me at least get my coffee and a bite to eat. How about an hour and a half?"

"Fine." Max hung up, and Stephanie hurried back to her bedroom to get dressed.

"Betsy, I have to hurry," she said as she went into the kitchen a few minutes later. Is Grandmother up?"

"Yes, she had some tea a few minutes ago. Miss Stephanie, it's only eight o'clock."

"So it is, Betsy. But I have to be way near Stanley by about nine thirty, and you know how I enjoy breakfast. I'll be back down in a minute or two."

She went up to her grandmother's room. Now was the time she had to tell her who Max was. She wasn't quite sure what the work he had for her involved, but she assumed it was something to do with his inheritance. How was she to tell her grandmother? Could she just say, Grandmother, Max Lamartine is Irwin Carmichael's nephew, and I'm going to work for him? No. It simply wouldn't work. But of course she couldn't lie about him. Not to her grandmother.

She could hold back the truth a little, though. Her grandmother didn't go out very much nowadays, and she probably wouldn't know who Max was, even now. Unless Mrs. Howard had told her. Mrs. Howard was just a little younger than her grandmother, and she knew everybody around. She came to see Mrs. Kimball once or twice a week, and they talked on the telephone nearly every day. But if Mrs. Howard had said anything about Max, Mrs. Kimball would surely have mentioned it long ago, before Max came in to help her after her fall. The door to her grandmother's room was open, and

Stephanie knocked lightly to gain her grand-mother's attention when she entered. Mrs. Kimball was propped up in bed, with the hot tea steaming on the bedside table.

"Good morning, Grandmother. I see you're having tea already."

"Yes, would you like some? I can get Betsy to bring it up."

"No, thank you. I'm having coffee downstairs in a few minutes. I wanted to tell you that I have a job now, and I have to leave as soon as I finish breakfast."

"Oh? Well, what sort of job is it?"

"I'm not really sure, Grandmother. It's something along the secretary line. Don't worry, it's only half days," she said, noticing that her grandmother's face fell ever so slightly when she announced her employment.

"Who are you working for?" asked her grandmother.

"I'm working for Max Lamartine. You remember, the man from last night, who brought me home from the dance. He seems to have a lot of paperwork connected with . . ."

"Yes, Betsy?" her grandmother interjected. Betsy had appeared at the door and was trying to get Stephanie's attention.

"I beg your pardon; Miss Stephanie is wanted on the telephone again."

"Oh," said Stephanie. "I'll leave you to your tea, then, Grandmother." The moment had been avoided when she had to tell her grandmother about Max's connection to Carmichael. But it was only a postponement, and Stephanie knew that soon she would have to summon up her will power again and tell her grandmother.

Marv Woods was on the telephone. "I just thought I ought to call you, Stephanie. You've been on my mind for the past day or so."

Stephanie preserved a meaningful silence.

"I know I didn't pay a lot of attention to you at the dance," he said in faltering words. "I'm sorry, but I ran into an old . . . friend. What happened to you when you went outside? I haven't gotten much of a picture of why that Mr. . . . is it Lamartine? . . . took you home, but . . ."

"Oh, it's nothing to worry about, Marv," she said. "Essentially unimportant. I'll have to tell you about it some other time, though, because I'm in quite a hurry just now. Goodbye, Marv."

She hung up. That was relatively easy, she thought. If only it were that easy to talk to Max.

She had hardly rung the bell when Max opened the heavy oak door.

"Ah, here you are," he said. "Thanks for coming so soon. I don't think you'll find the work very difficult at all. It involves typing out letters and in general getting some order into the chaos I've created in connection with the Carmichael estate."

She raised an eyebrow. "You see," he said, "I'm almost the only heir, but I'm executor of the estate too, and he had a lot of creditors. He was so much in debt to so many people and firms that it will be a miracle if I can ever straighten it out. Added to that, he was pressing for payment from a lot of people, and it seems questionable whether they actually owed him or not."

"You mean, you are involved with collecting bills Mr. Carmichael didn't really . . . wasn't really entitled to? I'm not sure I . . ."

"Nothing like that. You'll see when we get into that part of the work. It's a large can of worms. Actually I can't collect or pay very much anyway, because of legal tie-ups."

Max hit his open palm with his fist. "Sometimes I wish I could just wash my hands of the whole damn affair!"

He gave a little sigh, then collected himself. "Well," he said, smiling at Stephanie as he regained his composure, "I'm sorry I blew off a little steam there. Let's go in and I'll show you what I need done."

He ushered her into the sitting room, the same room in which she had taken sherry that first day she went to Stanley. Next to his desk was a smaller computer desk with some pencils and note pads. In between the two desks he had set up a work table, upon which Stephanie noticed several stacks of papers and some letter trays, along with a small file cabinet. The roll-top desk was, if anything more cluttered than when Stephanie saw it before.

Stephanie realized that Max's hand was on her shoulder. His touch was so gentle she hadn't known when he first touched her. She wanted to savor the delicate tingle his touch evoked. She turned to face him.

His lips were parted slightly, showing his perfectly even white teeth. She felt like a swimmer going under beneath his gaze. His dark eyes, hawkish under black brows, held her transfixed, and she seemed to lose herself—lose herself in the moment. All her emotions had been brought to the surface in a tiny slice of time.

As she looked in his eyes for that long moment, she was aware of a physical desire growing from somewhere in the region of the solar plexus, suffusing her entire body. The moment seemed to stand still, and she could sense a similar desire from him. Her mind was racing, and she required an effort of will to break away from the confusion that seemed to envelop her. She looked quickly away, realizing that within this man's glance lay danger.

"You'll take this desk," he said, guiding her to her chair as if nothing had passed between them. "To begin with, we need to go over these accounts to see how much is owed from the estate." He opened an accordion file as he spoke and brought out a large group of odd-sized statements.

Stephanie took her seat. "Then you'll want them separated into some sort of order, with totals, I suppose?"

"Yes. Perhaps we can put them in alphabetical order."

Stephanie worked by Max's side most of the morning, only stopping for occasional questions and for coffee. He was up and down to the telephone in the hallway.

"Remind me to have a telephone jack put in here for the desk," he said, almost absentmindedly, as he resumed his seat.

Stephanie took a sip of coffee, and was able to steal a glance at Max. She hadn't noticed the tiny slivers of gray curling round his ears before. He had an enigmatic face, with high cheekbones and a full lower lip that betokened a sensual nature. Had he sensed the tremor that thrilled through her body at his gentle touch earlier? She knew he had experienced a similar emotion, but would he admit it, even to himself? Or was it all fancy on her part—an everyday reaction by the gentler sex to this dark, appealing—yet forbidding—man of the world?

Dangerous. That was a word that kept coming to her mind as she looked at Max. But she couldn't explain how it applied to him.

She went back to her work—and it was quite a pile of bills she had to put in order. Then she was aware that he was scrutinizing her with an unabashed gaze. A shiver went down her back, and she felt the hair on her neck bristling.

"I'd like to know more about the beautiful, mysterious Stephanie Gray," he said. "So far everything you've told me would about fit in that coffee cup."

"Let's get one thing straight, <u>Mr</u>. Max Lamartine. I'm here on business, because you indicated you needed someone to help you out with these settlement papers." Her tone was defiant, and she thought for an instant that she had gone too far.

"But of course," she continued, "I do owe you several favors." Her voice had softened somewhat.

"And for some inexplicable reason, you want to prove yourself to me," he said.

Stephanie was indignant. She looked away from him with a haughty gesture. Then she glanced at him and saw a playful half-grin on his face. He was right, but she wasn't able to explain, even to herself, why she felt the need for his approval. In fact, she thought, I could find a lot about this dark, aloof man to dislike, if it weren't for the several times he has pulled me out of quicksand. Besides, for some reason just being with him has the strangest effect on me. Almost like repulsion and excitement at the same time.

"No matter," he said good-humoredly, relieving her of the slightly awkward moment, "it's about time to call it a day anyway. However, Miss Gray," he said teasingly, "I do expect you to be here at nine o'clock sharp in the morning."

He helped her from her chair. On the way to the door she came to the telephone stand. "Just a minute," she said, picking up the phone. She called the telephone company and requested an extension for Max at his desk.

"Wow!" he said. "That's efficiency for you. I had forgotten about the problem with the telephone. You're a sharp one."

"It's because of the nails I eat for breakfast," she replied. "Right now, I'm off the clock, though, and I'll be seeing you tomorrow."

Stephanie felt good about herself. On the way home she went over the day in her mind. She hadn't wanted this job. And she certainly wouldn't have thought about taking it except for her stupid pride! He had played his cards right when he suggested that she might not be capable. The very thought made her bristle. If there was one thing she thought about herself, it was that no one in the world was more capable of <u>anything</u> than she.

It was evident that Max wanted to become more intimately acquainted with her. But aside from the time he had held her briefly in his arms on the night of the dance, and when they both were carried away on the drive home, he hadn't offered to touch her beyond a normal gentlemanly gesture. He had certainly treated her with a lot more respect than Leon had.

She didn't even want to think about Leon and the way he had pawed at her. The thought of how he had planned to use her was revolting to her even now.

Max's touch, even the tiniest touch, was sensuous. It produced a reaction in her that she was almost at a loss to explain. He was a practiced lover, there could be no doubt about that. But he had never mentioned a woman or given her any inkling that he might have ever even gone out with a woman, or . . .

A terrible thought struck her. What if he were married, with five children at home! That would explain why he seemed so reserved around her. He was certainly old enough—she judged him to be about thirty. What an idea. It shouldn't concern her, but for some reason she felt stunned.

Stephanie could hardly sleep that night. When she did, it was to dream about Max, and in her dream she saw him standing at the door of his house, smiling at her. Strangely enough, he didn't say a word, but only beckoned for her to come in. When she did, he put his hand around her waist and looked deeply into her eyes. He said her name three times, and she felt a warm glow of contentment stealing over her body. She became fascinated with his mouth as he spoke. Then she looked into his eyes and suddenly realized that he was changed, and she was looking at Leon's leering face. Again he spoke, but this time it was Leon's voice.

"Stephanie," he said. "together, you and I can make it, and make it big."

She pulled away from him, and he kept looking at her. Then he said: "Don't do anything for him" pointing to Max behind her. "He's no good. He's a Carmichael!"

Stephanie had pulled away from Leon, and now he was across the room from her. He was grinning and laughing. He started walking toward her, and she felt the clutch of panic. Then she woke up.

She sat upright in bed and gave a little shudder. Thank heavens Leon was out of her life forever. She looked over at the clock: it was almost seven, and the alarm was just due to ring.

Somehow when Stephanie confronted Max at his house-turned-office that morning, she felt embarrassed, as if he could have been aware of her dream. Nonsense, she told herself.

"Did you sleep well last night?" he asked, giving her a start as she began to sort through the work on her desk.

"Of course I did," she lied. "Why do you ask?"

"I didn't mean anything by it, I was only making conversation. I hoped you had a good night's sleep so the work before us wouldn't tire you out. But you don't need to be so defensive. If you want me to, I'll just mind my own business."

Obviously he was bristling too this morning. "I'm sorry," she said. "I didn't mean to snap at you. I just . . . well, I really didn't sleep very well last night."

"I promise not to make you work too hard, then," he said. "I thought you looked as if the sleep had scarcely touched your eyelids. Still," he went on, "You look as beautiful, maybe even more beautiful, than you did yesterday."

Stephanie recalled Max's words at the service station, the first time she had seen him. He had said something about her lips inviting a kiss, and now she was aware that she would like a kiss from his lips at that moment. But she put it out of her mind and turned back to her desk.

Then his hand was brushing her face, and he was cupping her chin in his hand, and he was turning her face toward him. He leaned partly down to her, and she half rose from her chair. She felt as if he were drawing her up from her chair by an invisible string, and his lips were warm on hers, gentle, yet insistent, soft, yet demanding.

At first it was like the flash of the sun's rays on a dew-drenched leaf. It was almost as if his lips were yielding to hers, instead of the other way around. Then she felt his breath on her cheek. Almost instinctively she put her hand on his shoulder and was lifted from her chair as if by a magnet. His lips were exploring hers, sensuously moving in the excitement of discovery. He hadn't touched her with his hands except for that gentle touch on her face.

Stephanie couldn't stifle an almost inaudible sound that emanated deep in her throat. It was an encouragement to Max, and she felt his hand on the small of her back, drawing her against him. His fingertips still touched her face, and as she luxuriated in his kiss, she felt his fingers exploring her neck, gliding town to the top of her blouse.

Yet she didn't pull away from him. Two small voices seemed to whisper in her ear, one a warning, one an assurance. She listened to the assuring voice that told her to trust him. Ever so gently his fingertips touched the fullness of her breasts, and she thrilled to his touch.

"Stephanie," he said, as he relaxed the pressure of his lips on hers. "You excite me. You excite me as no other woman can."

She felt the roughness of his neck and realized that she had impulsively returned his embrace, gliding her arms around him as he drew her close against his body. The warning voice became more insistent, and she turned her head slightly to the side of his kiss. She wanted to cry "no" to him, but she could only mutter: "Oh, Max. Max. I think I had better get back to my work."

He stifled her words with his lips, and she felt his tongue delicately sending messages to her to forget about the work, to surrender to his kiss. But she knew she had to heed that warning voice, and she pulled away from him. She had never felt this way before, never experienced quite the feeling of surrender she had come so close to. But she knew it was the height of folly to give in to him, and she told herself that she must insist on simply a business relationship. She looked at Max and again the word "dangerous" intruded on her mind.

"I can't let you do this," she said. She didn't want to hurt his feelings, yet at the same time she had to keep him at a distance, partly because she didn't trust herself. "We have to keep ours a business relationship. You know, I don't know anything about you."

"I know even less about you," he countered.

"Well, in that case, we're utter strangers, aren't we?"

"Not utter," he quipped, "but almost utter. So tell me all about the beautiful and mysterious Stephanie Gray. To start with, I know some essentials, but you could find all that out from a resume. What I don't know is the inner Stephanie, the girl who comes all the way down from St. Louis to capture everybody's heart. Is there some young man back home you've given your heart and your vows to? And if there is, why aren't you wearing a ring?"

The questions were coming too fast for Stephanie, and she decided to ward them off.

"Those don't sound like questions concerning the trusteeship of an estate to me," she replied. "Maybe your words have a hidden meaning."

"The only thing hidden is the answer to my one question," said Max. "Why does this lovely creature come into my life from nowhere to torment me with her beauty?" He didn't want to let her break the spell. She didn't want to, either, but she felt she had no choice.

"I couldn't tell you the answer to that," she said, "but I can tell you this, boss"—she gave him a meaningful glance—"this printer needs a new ink cartridge."

"Okay for this time," he said, "you win this round. But I won't let up, Miss Gray." His tone was bantering. Then he narrowed his eyes and turned halfway toward Stephanie. "There will come a time, though," he said. "I always get what I want."

His words sounded ominous, but they made her tingle with a sudden excitement as she remembered the feel of his lips on hers. Partly to hide her embarrassment, she bent to her work.

The morning went quickly. The work was rather routine—accounts payable, some letters—and Stephanie got a lot done, Max working quietly at her side.

Next morning Max seemed preoccupied. He barely spoke to Stephanie before she took a break for coffee. Mrs. Roberts had the day off and Max brought Stephanie's cup in to her.

"Stephanie," he said, "how would you like to go with me over to Treasure Cove for dinner tonight? I won't pressure you if you don't want to, but it sure might be fun. I admit I'm getting a little restless here in Stanley. Small town life is great, but if you're used to the city as I am, you soon start wishing they didn't roll up the sidewalks at dusk."

He was echoing Stephanie's thoughts. If he hadn't put it like that, she would have turned him down. But she too was longing to be waited on at a fancy restaurant, and then perhaps a few cocktails at a piano bar, or an intimate corner table with soft lights and a combo playing.

"Do they have anything like that in Stanley or even in Greenville," she said, speaking her thoughts aloud.

"Anything like what, Stephanie?"

"Oh, I was just thinking out loud, Max. I was only thinking of the night life in St. Louis."

She frowned. "But that's in the past. No, I think I had better not accept, Max. I don't want to impose on you once again. God knows I've caused you enough trouble since I first saw you, and I don't want to put you out again."

Max compressed his lips in a comic expression, a caricature to her mind of a Samurai warrior. "Then I will pressure you," he said in a mock threat. Then, with a comical accent: *"I von't tak no for an answer, Mees Glay."*

Max looked so funny and his accent was so incongruous with his personality that Stephanie was forced to laugh. She knew he had found her weakness, for when she laughed like this she had no resistance to any suggestions, no matter how outrageous.

"What say, what say?" said Max, still in a nasal, high-pitched comic voice.

"Well, all right," returned Stephanie, between peals of laughter. "Only I have to warn you that I'm hard to please."

"Five thirty, then," said Max. "Now let's get back to work. What do you think I'm paying you for, eh?"

Five thirty came sooner than Stephanie realized it would, and she only just was ready when Max drove up. She didn't quite know where they were going—he had said Treasure Cove, but she didn't know where that was. She assumed it was one of the restaurants in Greenville.

Even so, she felt a little overdressed, in her tan suede suit. She had been dying to wear this outfit, but there's little chance to dress like this in Stanley. The jacket was unstructured, and the skirt was street length. She wore an ivory lace blouse with a low rounded neck, closed by tiny pearls. Her dark brown low-heel pumps matched her leather cummerbund and purse, and she completed her outfit with a topaz pin surrounded by seed pearls, matched by her dangle pearl earrings.

It was her hair that took the time. It fell in curls around the bottom, and she swept it back off her face to a French knot just behind the crown, showing off her earrings and her long neck. Tiny wisps of curls framed her face.

"I have reservations at Treasure Cove," said Max when he met her at the door. Then he stepped back to look at her. She knew her outfit was attractive, but she had still been anticipating his reaction with a little trepidation. And when he had spoken about the reservations, she was afraid he hadn't noticed her ensemble.

"Sensational! Just sensational. I knew you would be beautiful, but I never expected this. Just sensational. There's no other word for it."

"I hope I'm not overdressed," she said.

"No, not for Treasure Cove."

As he opened the car door for her, she noticed that he was dressed in a Harris Tweed jacket, with camel trousers and a silk shirt. His tie and handkerchief were silk.

"I've seen you on the dance floor," said Max unexpectedly, as he pulled into the road. "I'm hoping you'll enjoy some dancing after dinner."

"I sure would. You didn't say we were going dancing, but I'm glad we are."

Max turned off the road into the little Stanley airport, which had facilities only for small aircraft. He parked.

"Hammond is waiting," he said helping Stephanie from the car. "Let's go."

Holding Stephanie by the arm, he walked toward a small plane standing near the runway. She didn't have the time to ask the innumerable questions that came to mind.

"Ready, Max?" came a voice through a little speaker by the seat, as he and Stephanie were buckling on their seatbelts. Max picked up a little microphone from its clip by the speaker.

"Sure are, Hammond," he said. "Let's get moving."

As they lifted off the ground, Stephanie felt that sudden delightful sensation she always experienced when taking off in a plane. It was exhilarating. She caught her breath and, noting they were in a very comfortable six-seater, turned to Max.

"I feel like I'm being abducted," she said with a smile. "I've never gone on a dinner date quite like this."

"Only the best for you," replied Max with a smug look on his face.

"But you'll have to explain," she said. "I thought we were going to a little restaurant in Greenville. That's only about thirty five miles away."

"So you're wondering why we should take a plane." He smiled.

"Yes. You certainly didn't have to go to the expense and trouble of renting a plane."

"Renting a plane? I'm not renting a plane. I own it."

"You own it? Then who is Hammond?

"I should have explained. Eric Hammond is an employee of Lamartine Fabrics. You see, we constantly use air travel in my business, and I just have a pilot on the payroll. This happens to be my private plane, the one I use when I have to go to our offices in Bogotá, or the one in Calgary. If you look around you'll see this cabin is fitted up for fairly long flights. There's even a bunk over there for a catnap."

Stephanie was more amazed than ever. She hadn't realized until now just how wealthy Max was. Sure, he drove an expensive car, and he dressed expensively, though conservatively. But most middle-income people were able to afford an expensive look.

His manners went with his conservative dress and outward style. He spoke softly, and his movements were almost catlike in their grace and poise. He seemed to be considerate of others, and always treated everyone—at least so far as

Stephanie had observed—with equal friendliness and warmth. Except in the case of Jerry Osgood. Stephanie shivered at the thought of Jerry, and how he had humiliated her.

She had been looking out the window at the beautiful sunset, more breathtaking than ever from the air. Max caught her involuntary movement at the thought of Jerry Osgood.

"A penny for your thoughts," he said.

She turned to him and smiled. Indicating the view out the window to her right, she said, "I was just admiring the sunset—the blues and pinks, and—see the deep orange where the huge sun meets the horizon."

It was a thrilling sight, and Max leaned over her to get a better view. Doing so, he put his hand on her shoulder. She became aware that his face was very close to hers. Slightly turning her eyes, she noticed the contrast between his tan neck and the cream-colored silk shirt he wore. Her senses were filled with his musky masculinity. With a slight turn of his head, he brought his eyes in line with hers.

"Beautiful," he whispered, as he searched her eyes. "The sunset is beautiful, but it can't compare with you. 'For where is any author in the world, teaches such beauty as a woman's eye?' Shakespeare had it right."

Delicately he brushed her cheek with his fingers. Stephanie felt helplessly drawn to him. Her lips parted and she felt his breath warm on her cheek. Then his lips touched hers, and a growing desire impelled her to return the pressure of his lips. He was experienced in lovemaking, as his lips and hands told her. His tongue touched the fullness of her lips with electric, darting impulses. She was almost swooning, enveloped in an ecstatic glow. Then very gently she pulled her lips away from his.

"Oh, Max," she whispered, "you make me giddy."

He took encouragement from her response. He planted a string of tiny kisses on her cheek, and then she felt his tongue, soft as a butterfly's wing, touch her lips.

"About ten minutes more, Max!" It was Eric Hammond's voice over the speaker.

Max pulled away. "Look out the window again, Stephanie. That body of water is Lake Ponchartrain. We'll be landing soon."

"Lake Ponchartrain! So Treasure Cove is in New Orleans. I didn't have any idea . . . Max, I know it was a lot of trouble to arrange dinner at New Orleans!"

"Not really much trouble at all." He glanced at his watch. "You see, it's not even six thirty yet. And our reservations aren't until seven. So we'll have a leisurely drive over from the Lakefront Airport. I said nothing but the best for you."

He was right. There was a limousine waiting when they deplaned, and the drive took even less than a half hour. Treasure Cove was a large restaurant near The Cabildo.

"Ah, Mr. Lamartine," said a jovial-faced man as they entered, extending his hand.

Max shook his hand. "It's been a while, hasn't it, Tony?" He turned to Stephanie. "This is Tony Bellefonte. Stephanie Gray."

Tony smiled and made a little bow. "I hope you enjoy your dinner with us, Miss Gray. We have a table that may be perfect for you." He was ushering them to their table and seating them. "Never anything but the best for Max, and of course that extends to you."

As they took their seats he gave them a menu. "By the way, Max, I have a few vintage wines that aren't on the list. I'll get you my private list."

"You must come here often," said Stephanie, when Tony had gone. "Is he the owner?"

Max nodded. "Not really all that often— maybe once a month. I haven't been here in quite some time, though, but this is a special night."

To keep from feeling self-conscious, Stephanie looked around them. They were seated at a table near a large dance floor, and adjoining the floor was a small stage.

They had a cream sherry before dinner. Just as they finished their sherry the floor show began. A very attractive woman, clad in a black sequined outfit, sang to the accompaniment of a small orchestra. She began with "My Heart Will Go On," from "Titanic."

"Delightful," muttered Max, when the song was over. Stephanie also showed her approval by applauding. Their food had arrived. Max had chosen a light wine to go with their seafood, and the music and song were just the perfect touch to accompany their meal, without being too intrusive.

The music, the wine, the delectable food, the laughter they shared, all made for a lovely evening. Stephanie looked at Max, and was overwhelmed by his gaze. It was as if he were telling secret things with his eyes, communicating thoughts of love to her, and they were in a private world of their own making, away from the bustle of the diners in the restaurant.

Stephanie looked around her. The entertainer was singing, and Stephanie looked back at Max. He was totally engrossed in the singer and her song, "The Shadow of Your Smile":

"Now when I remember spring, all the joy
that love can bring, I will be remembering the
shadow of your smile."

She was singing the song to Max, and he was entranced by it. Stephanie looked at him.

"Her name is Marla," he said. "Marla O'Neal."

"Oh, you know her?"

"Yes, I do. I've known her for a long time," he said. Then he seemed to collect himself with a little shake of his head. "But I don't want anything to take away from our meal."

"In fact I'm about finished," she said.

"Then how about some espresso? Or a cognac?" He signaled to the waiter.

Stephanie took the cognac, and Max followed suit. The singer had taken a break, but the band began to play again.

Max asked Stephanie to dance. It was a slow foxtrot, and as he took her into his arms she felt that curious sensation of a current passing between them, just as she had felt so many times before.

"Max, I have to know some things about you. You are a mystery to me, and you remain a mystery, utterly incomprehensible."

Max smiled.

"I mean it. For example, I didn't know you owned a large business, or a plane, or anything like that."

"Didn't I tell you I was in business?"

"Yes, you did, but you only said something about being involved in a textile plant. I thought you might be some sort of executive. I didn't realize you owned the textile mill."

"Well, I don't quite own it. It's incorporated. I do own a controlling interest, though." He was silent a moment. "Did I pass that exam?"

"Yes, you passed," said Stephanie with a dreamy little smile. "But I have more."

"Fire away."

"It may seem like a silly question, but are you married?" She felt the blood throbbing in her temples.

"Would it matter?"

She pulled slightly away from him, trying to keep step. "Of course it would! I may be your modern girl, experienced and all that, but I'm not the sort to be going out with a married man." She tried to pull out of his grasp.

"Wait a minute, Stephanie. Calm down. I'm not married, for God's sake. I never have been. I'm just not the marrying kind, if I can use that old expression." He gathered her back into his arms, and they danced in silence.

"I'm sorry to be so inquisitive," she said after a minute. "It's just that I . . . I've never known anyone like you."

He held her close. "Stephanie, you go to my head," he whispered. "I don't have any secrets—I couldn't keep them from you anyway. So it doesn't matter if you're inquisitive. But it will be my turn next." He looked at her with a meaningful expression.

She felt secure in his arms, hoping the dance wouldn't end. But it did, and she led the way back to the table where a slip of paper was waiting on a tray at Max's place.

"Oh, I'm sorry, I have a phone call," he said, glancing at the note.

Left to herself at the table, Stephanie reflected on the events of the day. This morning she was only working for this man, this dynamic personality, helping him out with some of the work involved with his trusteeship of his uncle's estate. He had kissed her, and inexplicably insinuated himself into her emotions. She had been able to handle that. Now it appears that he is not just a friend, not just an unimportant person who needed a little secretarial help, but a major figure in industry, an important person who calls the shots wherever he goes, and who is known all over the country.

And he was playing a game with her heart, a game in which, no matter what she did, she could only be the loser.

Leon had taken advantage of her. He had used her to try to rise in business circles, to build an empire, no matter how petty, of his own favoritism bought by her influence. Luckily she saw through him in time. On the other hand, Max didn't need her influence—not that she had any since her father died. But Max was attracted to her, that was obvious. And it was a mutual attraction. Still, she could only suppose that he wanted to use her to satisfy his own desires, and would soon tire of her and cast her off.

"You are sitting with Max?" The singer, Marla O'Neal, had approached Stephanie's table. "Do you mind if I join you for a moment? I'm an old friend of Max."

"Well, of course, please join us," replied Stephanie with a tiny smile. She was slightly puzzled. Max had said he knew her, but hadn't elaborated. At that moment Max came up to the table.

"Marla! How nice to see you." He kissed her on the cheek. "You've met Stephanie?"

Marla looked briefly at Stephanie. "Stephanie Gray. This is Marla O'Neal," said Max smoothly.

"Take a seat, Marla. Will you have anything? No? Not while you're working."

Suddenly Stephanie realized that Max's effusiveness was sounding self-conscious, completely out of character for him. But then, what is in character for him? He was a man full of surprises, and Stephanie couldn't predict what he would do or say from one minute to the next.

"I enjoyed your singing very much, Marla," said Stephanie. "Do you sing here regularly?"

"Yes I do, as a matter of fact. Tuesday through Saturday. Thanks for the compliment."

She turned to Max. "Well, Max, it's been ages since I've seen you." She put a hand on his arm. "I hope you haven't forgotten how we made the rounds of the French Quarter at Mardi Gras—those were the days."

Max cleared his throat. "Marla, are you sure you don't want anything? I'd be happy to order for you."

"Thanks, no," she said.

He looked at his watch. "But I'm afraid the guys in the band are looking for you now. Thank you for the songs."

"Sure, Max, sure," she said. "I'll dedicate this next one to you"—she turned slightly to Stephanie, "and to your girl friend here."

She got up to leave. Before she did so, she came up close to Stephanie and grasped her hand. In a whisper she said, "Be careful."

Max was turned to look at the band, and didn't hear Marla's words. He looked back to Stephanie. "I'm afraid we'll have to cut our evening a little short," he said. "That phone call was from Lorraine Pringle at my office. I suppose I ought to tell you that I'm trying to negotiate a merger with another firm, and things are starting to break. One of the principals in the arrangements has been trying to get in touch with me. I placed a call to him just now, but he's not available."

"None of that would have anything to do with our evening, except that I need to have a little confab with my chief attorney, Neils Patterson, yet tonight." He gave Stephanie a helpless look. "So you see, I'm not master of my own time right now. I do apologize."

"It's all rather exciting, though," said Stephanie. "Isn't it? Probably as exciting as hearing Marla O'Neal sing love songs to you."

"Now wait a minute," he said. "In the first place, I didn't say we had to leave right now. In fact, I'd like to dance this next one with you. In the second place, that remark about Marla was really uncalled for. She never meant that much to me, even though we . . . we were very good friends, and still are. It's an old friendship."

He looked earnestly at her, but she kept her eyes averted.

"So how about this dance?" he asked.

Stephanie couldn't help feeling miffed, even though she knew she was being unfair. A tiny pout was on her mouth.

"No, I'm afraid I don't feel much like dancing. Besides that," she added, "are you sure it's all right with Miss Pringle for you to dance? I suppose we should leave right now, seeing that she's so anxious to get you back."

Max didn't reply, but stood up abruptly and reached over to help Stephanie from her chair. He had a cold expression on his face.

"In that case we'll go," he said. He signed the bill and gave it to the waiter with an expression of his thanks to him and to Tony.

As they stepped out into the windy night Stephanie told herself that she had been too quick to blame. Looking at Max as he held the door of the limousine for her, she had an apology on the tip of her tongue. But his expression was rocklike and grim, and she told herself that she just couldn't apologize, couldn't abase herself to this proud man.

Still, Max was politeness personified. They drove to the airport and boarded the plane in silence.

It wasn't until Stephanie had settled back in Max's car at Stanley that she felt she could hazard some sort of speech. She had to say something to him!

"Max, please don't think I meant any criticism of your private life, or of the company you keep. I certainly don't have any right to pry into your personal relationships . . . I mean, just because you asked me out doesn't mean you can't go out with whomever you please, whenever you please. I mean . . . oh, I don't know what I mean."

Max didn't alter his expression.

She continued, "I just don't want you to think there's anything in our relationship, anything more than just a date. I don't want to get serious about anybody now; God knows I've had . . ."

Max looked at her sharply. She couldn't go on. She was thinking about Leon Ainsworth, and her emotions were on her sleeve. She didn't want to say anything about Leon to Max, though. In regard to Leon she wanted to let sleeping dogs lie.

"You've had what?" he asked. "I'm sure you aren't the lily white girl you seem, Stephanie. And I'm equally sure you have a past of some sort." He paused and shook his head. "But I don't want to know about it. Keep it to yourself. I prefer to think of you just as you are, beautiful, mysterious, a little naive and a little petulant, but above all, wholesome and desirable."

To prevent herself from blushing Stephanie lashed out at him.

"A past? Yes, I have a past. One I prefer not to discuss, <u>Mr</u>. Lamartine. But I'm sure it's nothing to the past you've had—Marla O'Neal, Lorraine Pringle, God knows how may other women, all beautiful and sexy just like Marla O'Neal is."

During her outburst Max had slowed and pulled over onto the shoulder of the road. Now he reached over and took her arm with his hand, pulling her up against him. With a single action he stifled her speech with his mouth, heavy on hers.

She was enveloped by his muskiness, by his overpowering aura. Without realizing what she was doing she reached her hand up around his neck to feel the now familiar texture of his skin. She slid her hand in between the silk shirt and his neck and around to meet his hairline. His hair was coarse in her fingers, providing a contrast to the softness of his skin.

At the same time she felt his hand on her stomach, sliding up to touch her breasts under her lace. This time she didn't try to stop him. This man represented a danger to her in many ways, but she couldn't stop to analyze them now. She only knew at this moment that she desired him, and that she was surrendering herself to what seemed inevitable.

Deftly he undid the pearl buttons that led to her throat, and his hand traced sensuous patterns on her skin beneath her blouse. His hands and lips were impetuous, conquering her resistance. As he stroked her breasts and probed her lips with his tongue, he awakened that desire in her that she hadn't felt since breaking off with Leon.

Max had taken off his jacket to drive, and she undid his tie with an easy motion. In no time his shirt was open to the waist, and she felt his bare chest heaving with his demand and his desire. There was no holding back for Stephanie now. Tonight she would surrender her body to him. Together they would fulfill their mutual passion.

"Stephanie, Stephanie, you're maddening," he whispered. He loosened her cummerbund, and her suede skirt slid off under his gentle insistence. He had found the exquisitely sensitive places on her skin, and she moved to bring her torso against his hard body.

Suddenly the name Marla intruded on her thoughts. Why must that woman loom before me now? she thought.

She was caught between desire and revulsion. She wanted this man to take her, wanted it more than she had ever wanted anything, but at the same time she heard those words repeated over in her head: be careful! Marla had said. And simultaneously that image of Leon came to her, leering at her as in her dream. She pushed against Max's chest.

"No, Max, we mustn't."

"What—for God's sake, Stephanie, what is it?"

"It's just that—we can't do this. We can't go on." She knew he wouldn't understand her reasons, wouldn't care to understand.

"I don't want it," she said. "I don't have that desire, Max." She lied to him to make him stop his lovemaking.

"Stephanie, you know I can't resist you now. I want you. I want you to come home with me tonight."

"Spend the night with you? And in the morning? Think about it, Max. It just won't work out."

That was exactly the way Leon had approached the subject of sex with Stephanie. The memory was all too vivid in her mind. Hastily she dressed and put her hair in order.

"Dammit, Stephanie. For a minute there I thought you wanted me as much as I wanted you. Either that or you were acting a part. And if you were, you're a good actress." He was buttoning his shirt.

She couldn't deny it to herself, she had wanted him. But it wouldn't do to let him know it. He could very easily take advantage of her desire. She bit her lip in her frustration. She couldn't afford to break down now. She had committed herself to making him think she didn't want him, didn't desire him, when actually she had wanted him with every fiber of her being.

But that black cloud had come between them. Marla, Lorraine Pringle, Leon—even Irwin Carmichael's ghost stood between them. There were just too many arguments against an impetuous relationship with Max.

"Well, I'm not acting a part. I don't mean to hurt your feelings, Max, but no thanks. I can't spend the night with you, tonight or any other night. And if that's reason to fire me, then fire away."

That may have been the very reason he hired me, she thought. So he was just another one of those men who wanted to use his power to force me into his bed. Well, it won't work.

"I certainly won't fire you," he said as he pulled the car into the highway. "Take the day off tomorrow—I have to be in Memphis tomorrow and over the weekend. But be sure to show up Monday at the regular time. We still have plenty of work to do."

Six

Memphis

What dreams Stephanie had dashed to the ground! She felt thrust back into the round of existence that consisted of her bedroom at her grandmother's, her car, the fields of late corn, the people and personalities that comprised her circle. What a contrast this daily round was to the almost dreamlike evening she had experienced with Max—until she cut it short by her jealousies and doubts.

Nola came on Sunday, and she and Stephanie had a long talk. Stephanie told her what Irwin Carmichael had done to her grandfather, and how she held a resentment against Max because of Carmichael.

"You can't hold Max responsible for his uncle's misdeeds," said Nola. "If justice were administered like that, very few people would be out of jail."

"Maybe so, but you don't know the extent of Carmichael's wrongdoing. I don't know if you've heard about Doreen?"

"I think I have," replied Nola. "Doreen Fletcher. Wasn't she a prostitute? She was pretty notorious for some reason years ago, but I don't remember the circumstances."

"I heard about her from my grandmother," said Stephanie. "The story I got was that she literally ran the town from that bar over by the Cotton Exchange building. She must have made a pile of money, and she made it by goading Carmichael into all the evil things he did to people. I only know what he did to my grandfather, but I'm sure he took a lot of other people for a cleaning too."

"Yes, he did." said Nola. "But that doesn't really have anything to do with Max, does it?"

"I don't know whether it does or not. I have a funny feeling about it, though."

"I remember about Doreen now," said Nola. "I understand that when she left Carmichael, she left with most of his money—what she could lay hands on in negotiables. He was pretty careless when it came to his own money. He kept most of it in cash."

"Why did he do that?"

"Because he had done so many things to so many people, he figured if anyone ever got a line on him, or could prove anything against him, he'd be able to run with his money. He had it hidden in various places. Doreen found out where most of it was, and took it with her when she left."

"What about his property?" asked Stephanie.

"He didn't have a clear title to about half of it."

"I guess I knew that—I'm having to do a lot of title searches now."

"And the rest of it, well, you know what's happening to it, I suppose," said Nola. "I imagine the Carmichael estate owes a lot of money."

"How well I know."

"So what Max is inheriting—and you can correct me if I'm wrong—is not a lot of substance but a lot of indebtedness."

"Of course the house is worth a lot."

"Sure. But Stephanie, he'll probably have to liquidate that for the money to pay off the debts."

"I guess I never thought of it that way," said Stephanie. "I had looked on it as ill-gotten gains, with Max as the beneficiary—almost as if he were a partner to Carmichael's crimes."

"I just think you're wrong about Max, Stephanie. Of course, you know him a lot better than I do." She gave Stephanie a suggestive look.

"Now Nola," said Stephanie with a devilish grin, "don't you go jumping to conclusions. As far as I'm concerned it's only an employer-employee relationship."

"Sure. And pigs have wings, too."

"Well, I have to admit our dinner date was a date to make anyone envious. Even you. I couldn't believe that plane! Six seats, with plush up-holstery—he even has a bunk to nap on when he's on a long trip."

"How convenient," said Nola with half-closed eyes.

Stephanie turned pink.

"I have a good idea," said Nola. "Let's go for a swim. We can swim over at the country club, if you don't have any other plans."

They spent the rest of the afternoon at the country club, swimming and sipping soft drinks. Afterward they had dinner with Jeff at Nola's house.

Stephanie was up early the next morning. She was eager to get on with her work for Max, and though she didn't want to admit it to herself, she was looking forward to seeing him.

Max's house looked strangely desolate when she drove up at nine. She was on the point of ringing the doorbell when she noticed a brass hasp had been placed on the door with a padlock. A printed note was also tacked onto the door which read: "This property has been sealed off pending litigation pursuant to claims made upon the estate of Irwin Carmichael, deceased."

Stephanie was amazed, and she didn't know what to do. She went back to her car, and sat there for a moment. As she reached in her purse for her cell phone, she heard a car pull in behind her. It was Max.

"You look puzzled." He was smiling.

"I am puzzled," she replied. "How am I to get anything done if all my work is locked up in that house? And why is it locked, anyway? I don't understand it."

"Calm down," he said. "Didn't you read the sign? Somebody is filing a counter-claim for the house. Uncle Irwin didn't have a very good will—let me correct that, he didn't have a legal will at all, and I'm apparently not the only person who can file for his inheritance. But pull your car over to the store and lock it. We'll go for coffee and talk about what to do next."

Stephanie parked at the little lot beside the general store. She slid in beside Max and he drove down the highway two or three miles past Jerry Osgood's house to a little cafe. Over their coffee Max explained the circumstances.

"Somebody else has a claim on Uncle Irwin's property—or thinks she has. You see, I'm not related to Uncle Irwin by blood. He was married to my maternal aunt, who passed on several years ago. But this woman lived with him for a time—I don't know how long—and she thinks she has a right to his inheritance. Just between you and me, I almost wish she did, because at this point it looks like he had more debts than can ever be paid off with the value of his property."

"Is her name Doreen?"

"Yes. Doreen Fletcher. How did you know?"

"Oh, I've heard about her, Max. I know more about her and your uncle than you might think."

"Then tell me, for God's sake. What kind of claim does she have?"

"Well, I'm not sure about that. In fact, I didn't think she'd even try for a counter-claim, because she doesn't seem to have any rights whatsoever to your uncle's effects."

"On what basis is she filing then? What do you think her claims are?"

"Now you have to realize, Max, that everything I say is only secondhand information—

hearsay, and I can't verify anything. In fact, Nola and my grandmother told me most of what I'm telling you."

"Well, you've already told me more than I've been able to learn on my own. Everything I've found out has been from the clerk of courts—and the people there don't want to tell me anything. I don't know why, Stephanie, but I seem to be unpopular around here."

A little twinge of conscience made Stephanie bite her lip. Still she didn't know how to treat Max in regard to his uncle. It was obvious that people in Stanley were bitter toward Irwin Carmichael's memory just like she was.

"I don't know a lot about Doreen, Max, but I do know that she lived with your uncle for about a year. She had been a prostitute, and apparently she manipulated your uncle into some pretty shady deals. The way I heard it, they ran the town together from Wilson's bar. When she left your uncle, she took most of his money, which he kept in cash."

"In cash? That wasn't very smart. That explains why he didn't have much money in his bank account. Why did he keep cash?"

"Max, you might not know the extent of your uncle's shady dealings," ventured Stephanie. "In fact, it was so people couldn't put the bite on any of his assets legally. I also suspect his relationship with the IRS was on pretty shaky ground."

Max widened his eyes in understanding. "That explains a lot, Stephanie. I had no idea . . . so that's why those property titles are so mixed up. I wouldn't be surprised to find that many of them are worthless."

He paused a minute and stared into his coffee cup. Stephanie thought he looked a little deflated, and a little forlorn. Her heart went out to him at his next words.

"I don't know if you still want to work for me, Stephanie. I didn't realize it was quite this . . . bad. Or this complicated. But I still want you."

He looked into her eyes. His words made her shiver with excitement until she came to her senses. He was only saying he wanted her to work for him.

"Of course I want to," she replied. "But we can't get into the house, can we?"

"No, we can't, but that's all right. I took out all the papers and other materials we need, with the approval of the court. We have another problem, though. I've sent everything to Memphis. Is there a possibility that you could take a small apartment in Memphis? I'll compensate you for the extra expense in rent. I have an office at the mill that can be fixed up just for you. What do you say?"

"Well, you can get somebody else right there in Memphis, can't you?"

"No one who knows the work at this point like you do."

"Besides that, I would have to leave my grandmother and Betsy for an extended time." She knitted her brows. "My first inclination is to say no, Max."

"Please."

What could she say? It was a business proposal, and there was not really any reason she couldn't move to Memphis. Maybe she was afraid. Afraid to find out what Max's life was like in Memphis. She knew he kept busy—she suspected he was with a different woman every night. But what he did with his private life was his business, and she refused to let herself become intimidated by such notions.

"All right. You'll have to give me a little time to pack."

"How about driving up on Wednesday? I can make arrangements for a furnished apartment today."

So once again Stephanie packed. She wasn't expecting to be in Memphis over a week or two, so she didn't require much in the way of clothing.

But she had to face her grandmother, and she knew Mrs. Kimball wouldn't like the idea of her leaving, especially when she had only been living there so short a time. But to her surprise Mrs. Kimball gave her blessing.

"As long as I'm sure that Mr. Lamartine will be . . . looking after you, then my mind will be at ease. But Stephanie, you never have told me just who Mr. Lamartine is—what he's doing here in Stanley. Is he here on business?"

This was it. She couldn't lie to her grandmother.

"Well, yes, he is here on business of a sort. First let me tell you that Mr. Lamartine is a very fine person, Grandmother. Not only that, but he is extremely wealthy." She was already on the defensive, taking up for Max before she had cause.

"Money doesn't always guarantee strength of character, by any means, Stephanie," said her grandmother matter-of-factly.

"Yes, I know," said Stephanie. "But Max has strength of character, you know that, Grandmother. You've only seen him a couple of times, but I'd be willing to bet that you have an opinion of him already." She was hedging on the issue of who Max was.

"My opinion is that he's a fine young man," replied her Grandmother. "But that doesn't tell me who he is."

"Well, Grandmother, he's Irwin Carmichael's nephew." She didn't look at her grandmother. "His nephew by marriage. His mother was Estelle Carmichael's sister. And he's here because of the court matter over Mr. Carmichael's inheritance."

Mrs. Kimball's face was immobile. The silence in the room was oppressive, but Stephanie couldn't bring herself to say any more. She had made the case—the only case that could be made for Max: that he wasn't a blood relative to Irwin Carmichael.

Mrs. Kimball's expression remained impassive. Without turning, she asked between thin lips, "How did he acquire his wealth?"

"His father was in the fabric business in Memphis, and Max has built that business up until it's a world-wide concern, now. He's a major stockholder."

Mrs. Kimball turned to face Stephanie. "Just what are his intentions toward you? I know he wants you to work for him, but is that all? He's certainly not blind to the fact that you are a very attractive young woman."

"Oh, Grandmother, he doesn't have any sort of romantic ideas about me. Sure, he flirts with me, but it's only in fun. And he took me out because it was something to do."

"Flying you to New Orleans for dinner doesn't sound like a casual date to me."

Stephanie hadn't thought of it that way. "I told you he has more money than he knows what to do with. He probably flies to New Orleans often."

"Sounds like what I would call a spendthrift," said Mrs. Kimball.

Stephanie had no answer for this.

"But that part doesn't matter," continued Mrs. Kimball. "What does matter is that you do what you think is best. I'm sure we can manage without you for a while, Betsy and I."

Stephanie arrived in Memphis at the appointed time and went directly to the apartment Max had rented. He was waiting for her in the parking lot.

"I hope you like this," he said as he opened the door for her. "I had someone at the office rent it for you, and I haven't seen it yet myself."

The apartment looked a lot more sumptuous than Stephanie had expected. "I hope it didn't cost too much," she said. "I suppose it's rented by the week?"

"Yes," he replied. "And for the cost, don't worry about that—I can write it off to expenses."

Stephanie didn't know what to reply, and she just stood looking at this commanding personality who had entered her life in such a haphazard way. She was aware of the inexplicable feeling that there was a bond between them, that whatever he did she would go along with because he had some sort of hold on her, not an unpleasant hold like Leon had had, but something—something that seemed to draw her to him. It was almost like a curious form of thought-transference, a pleasurable mental hold that she couldn't combat, even if she had felt herself able to combat it.

He was searching her face and her body with his eyes. Then by what seemed to be a force of will he broke the spell.

"It's time for dinner, and I suppose you are tired. I'll give you a little time to freshen up and then we'll go to dinner. I promise not to take you to New Orleans."

She laughed. "That's very considerate of you, Max. I mean your offer to take me to dinner. But it's all right, I can get something somewhere—there's that fast food place across the street."

"Nonsense. I'll just go down to the corner for the paper and you can change—not anything too dressy, now, because we'll just go to a little cafe nearby for a bite."

A relaxing meal in a small cafe was just what Stephanie needed, and the meal itself was delicious. On the way back Max showed her some of the landmarks of Memphis just to help her become oriented. He said he would pick her up the next morning, so he could introduce her around and show her where everything was at the mill, promising to take her on a short tour of the mill at the same time.

The morning couldn't come too soon for Stephanie. She was up at the first light and was ready to go when he came.

Together they went up a brief set of steps and through some heavy glass doors marked <u>Lamartine Fabrics</u>. <u>General</u> <u>Offices</u>. Then down a carpeted hallway to a large and elegantly furnished office. Behind the desk sat a pleasant woman Stephanie took to be in her mid-fifties, who looked up at them from the mahogany reception area. Her cheerful face was made even more cheerful by the butterfly-shaped glasses she wore. She smiled at Stephanie and Max.

Stephanie suppressed her impulse to laugh at her own folly—she had thought Lorraine Pringle was probably someone young and vivacious, someone like Marla O'Neal. To hide her embarrassment she greeted Miss Pringle with effusiveness.

"It's my pleasure to meet you, Stephanie," said Lorraine Pringle. "Please call me Lorraine. I have an idea we'll get on famously. In fact, Mr. Lamartine has told me to show you around the offices."

Max had disappeared into an inner room, and Lorraine rose from her chair. She showed Stephanie where the executive offices were, and where her own office would be. She introduced Stephanie to some of the staff, who were cordial and seemed eager to help Stephanie any way they could. Finally Lorraine took her to Max's office, and went back to her desk.

"I'm very impressed, Max. Even more impressed than I was by your private plane."

Max smiled at the compliment. "Come on, then," he said, "and we'll see some of the rest of the operations of the mill. I promised to show it to you."

The brief tour lasted about an hour. Max explained various operations to Stephanie. She was intrigued by the carding and weaving operations, and amazed at the results obtained in the dyeing and finishing departments. Last of all he took her up a metal staircase to the roof, where he showed her the company helicopter.

"Eric Hammond has charge of this baby," he said with evident pride. "We just acquired this 'copter a couple of months ago."

"What do you use it for?"

"Our executives have to travel frequently from here to the airport, and even more often to our other mill across town."

Stephanie was favorably impressed by the whole operation. It didn't take her long to settle in to her work, and she found that she was able to get a lot done in a short time.

On Friday after work she was just preparing to leave her office when Terry Sells, one of the junior executives, came in.

"How do you like it here by now?" he asked with a smile.

"Fine, Terry. The work isn't very difficult, and everyone has been nice to me."

"You're from St. Louis, aren't you?"

"Yes, I am. How did you know?"

"Word gets around. They also say you're un-attached, and . . ."

"And what?"

"Oh, nothing. It's just gossip."

"Now that you've mentioned it you'll have to tell me."

He had a stupid look on his face, as if he wished he hadn't said anything. "They say . . . well, that you're Max's girl. None of us other poor slobs have a chance with you."

Stephanie bristled. She had only gone out with Max one time, that is, one time on a real date, and now gossip had it that she was "his girl." Well, she would put a stop to that.

She smiled her sweetest smile at Terry. "The very idea! I'm certainly not 'Max's girl,' or anybody else's. And I suspect you're not a poor slob after all, but probably a very sweet one."

He laughed, and Stephanie could see he was relieved. She had noticed how outgoing Terry was when she met him that first morning on her tour. Since then he had flirted with her a little, and she had an idea he was going to ask her out. But she didn't know he was held back by the notion that she was Max's girl.

"Stephanie, it turns out that I've been invited to a picnic tomorrow, and I should bring someone. You see, I'm a member of a gourmet club that meets for a shared dinner once a month, and this month they've planned a picnic. Would you like to go?"

"Well, this is so sudden," said Stephanie. She batted her eyes in a theatrical gesture.

"I guarantee the food will be superb. Every member has to contribute something to the picnic, and I'm bringing a mocha cheesecake that is out of this world."

"You're making my mouth water. What time is the picnic?"

"They usually plan it for around five-thirty, but it's better to go a little early—about five. So I could pick you up around a quarter till. What do you say?"

"All right, Terry. It sounds like fun."

Terry was right on time. Stephanie had never been to a gourmet club picnic, so she didn't know quite what to expect. She knew her appetite would be satisfied. She also knew she would have a good time, because Terry had such a friendly personality. And she had an idea that among the ranks of gourmets was to be found a wide range of interesting people. So it promised to be enjoyable.

She wore a rather casual pants suit with a sash around her waist. She wanted to look the part of an epicure, but wasn't quite sure how to do it, so she copied one of the models in an issue of a gourmet magazine she found on the newsstand. She copied it even to the hairdo pulled over one shoulder. The effect must have been stunning because Terry's reaction was even better than she had hoped.

"Stephanie, you look fantastic," he said, when she met him at the door.

"I hope that's a compliment, and I accept it," she said with a smile as she held her hand out to him. He kissed her hand, blushing as he did.

How different he is from Max, she thought. If Max had kissed her hand it would have been a completely natural gesture, but Terry acts like he's playing a part. But I can forgive him for being a little self-conscious.

She did have a good time as Terry had promised she would. But she found herself looking around, expecting to see Max's familiar broad shoulders in the crowd. Once she nearly said something to someone who looked like Max from the back. He turned around just in time, and she saw he was the host of the picnic, whom she had met at their arrival.

"Are you enjoying yourself, Stephanie?" he asked. Stephanie was trying to remember his name. Just as he introduced his wife, Dorothy, it came to her. Allen. Allen Dodge.

"It's a pleasure to meet you, Dorothy. Allen has been telling me how you are the star of these get-togethers. What is it you provided this time? Besides the excellent wine, I mean."

Dorothy was the shadow of her husband. She was as proud as he was of the way they had arranged the picnic. "Have you had the shish kabob?" she asked. "It is a specialty of the Allen Dodges."

And so it went. The picnic was a success, from Allen Dodge's standpoint, and it was a success from Terry Sells' standpoint. Stephanie enjoyed herself, but at the same time she realized that she was a little lost among those who were members of the club. It was almost as if the picnic were divided between the members and the non-members— friends, dates—and the non-members didn't quite know what was going on. They seemed in a daze.

Terry was wearing a blazer with a fancy emblem on the breast, and white shoes. His black moustache, trimmed to perfection, set off his white teeth.

As they talked to the various people at the picnic, Stephanie realized that Terry Sells' main objective in life was to make a good impression on everyone. He used carefully studied and stylized gestures. The fact that he was so interested in his effect on people probably went a long way toward explaining his relative success as a marketing executive.

Taking their leave of the people at the picnic, Terry touched Stephanie's arm in an almost proprietary fashion. Stephanie suddenly realized that her function was the same as his blazer, or his duck trousers, or his white shoes. She was, in a manner of speaking, a decorative object.

That knowledge didn't take away from her enjoyment of the picnic. The various gourmet items were delectable. She enjoyed Terry's company just as much as she would have if she hadn't realized how he viewed her. But still she hoped he wouldn't draw out their evening together.

It was almost eight thirty when they walked to his car, which he had pulled off the shell road that adjoined the park in which the picnic was set up.

"Would you like to go for cocktails, Stephanie?"

"If you don't mind, Terry, not this time. I've had a great time." She could tell that was what he wanted to hear. "I'm not used to late hours, though, and early as it is still, I want to turn in before too long."

He didn't press her, and she suspected he had only asked her because he thought it was the proper thing to do. She stole a glance at him, sitting behind the wheel of his perfect BMW, with his perfect moustache below his perfectly shaped nose, and she thought how much he was like a storybook hero. But he wasn't the flesh and blood hero she would have dreamed of. Like Max, for example.

Max was also something of a storybook hero, but he was all man, with such imperfections as flesh and blood men have. He was older than Terry, and Stephanie had the feeling that somehow Terry would never have quite the maturity, maturity born of experience—possibly wisdom was the word—that Max had.

She enjoyed being with Terry, though. He was a perfect gentleman, and he let her into her apartment without the slightest suggestion of wanting to take her in his arms or kiss her. She was grateful for that, because she was certainly not interested in starting anything with him.

"I'll see you on Monday, then," he said, and with that simple statement was gone—comfortable, safe in the knowledge that his date had been perfect.

Stephanie usually came to work a little later than the mill employees did, and when she showed up at nine o'clock Monday morning, Lorraine Pringle greeted her in her friendly way. Lorraine had the information that Stephanie's date with Terry was general knowledge by now. Evidently Terry was anxious to advertise that he had taken out the beautiful temporary clerk, as Lorraine put it, within days of her first coming to Lamartine Fabrics.

"Where is Terry now?" asked Stephanie. She hadn't seen him in his office when she passed.

"He was in about an hour ago, but had to go out on a marketing visit to one of his accounts. He probably won't be back until late afternoon."

"Oh, swell. Lorraine, I want to set the record straight. I went out with him, yes, but it was a very casual date, and I don't want anybody around here thinking anything about it. Sure I like Terry, but I went because it was a very interesting picnic. I like everybody around here."

She paused. "Besides that, it's nobody's damn business what I do on my own time." She was getting a little too worked up, and she knew it.

Lorraine was quick to try to smooth things over. "Okay, okay. Don't worry, Stephanie. Nobody's anxious to create anything out of your personal life."

"I'm sorry I blew up. I wonder why Terry spread that around."

"I suppose he's proud of it. Terry's like that. You'll see."

Stephanie went to her desk. She was beginning to feel miserable. What if Max had heard the gossip? How would he take it? Strangely enough, when she thought of Max she felt her skin tingle.

Suddenly she looked up. There stood Max in the door to her office, his hand on the door frame. He wasn't smiling.

"Come into my office for a minute."

She went into Max's office, and he closed the heavy oak door behind her. It seemed to take an excruciatingly long time for him to walk around his desk to take his seat. Stephanie remained standing.

Max's face, his whole manner, was menacing. "How do you like our plant by now?"

"Very nice. Everyone has been swell to me."

"Yes, I know. I've heard how anxious people are to show you the sights.

"What do you mean by that?"

"One of our junior executives seems to have taken you over. I think he wants to add you to his collection."

"Oh, you mean Terry."

"Yes, I mean Terry." Max's face was inscrutable.

"Add me to his collection? What do you mean? Does he have a collection . . . of women?"

"No, not women. Terry doesn't even know any women. Or rather, none know him. He collects—collectibles."

It was obvious to Stephanie that Max was making an effort to control his temper. He gritted his teeth.

"But I'm not a collectible!" she said. The situation was becoming less and less humorous.

"And I don't want you to become one!" Max said. He assumed that manner that told Stephanie she was being dismissed.

She didn't want to go. She wanted to offer a rebuttal, to tell him he couldn't order her around, couldn't interfere in her personal life. Rumor had pounced on her from both sides—first by saying

Max possessed her, and now by implying that she was in some way being used by Terry Sells like one of his personal decorations. And she hadn't even been in Memphis a week yet.

But she couldn't stand up to Max, not in this. She wanted to scream at him that he couldn't order her around, that she would date whomever she pleased; but the alternative seemed in her confusion to be that she become known as part of Terry's perfect world, one of his objects, to be admired by one and all.

She clenched her fists and spoke between her teeth. "Why does a simple afternoon picnic have to turn into an espionage affair?" she said into the air.

Max didn't answer. He simply turned away from her with a haughty look which invited her to leave his office. She turned and left without a word.

Stephanie was free to set her own hours, and she waited until the offices were cleared out for lunch, and then shut her office door and went home.

By the time she arrived at her apartment she had cooled off somewhat. She had to walk through a covered walkway, lined with mailboxes, to reach her apartment door. As she stepped onto the cement she conceived the feeling that someone was following her. She stopped and listened, but didn't hear anything. Then she resumed walking, and . . . there it was again! She was near her door. She definitely heard footsteps behind her, but when she glanced back she couldn't see around the corner of the building into the walkway. It wouldn't be Max? Her heart beat faster.

Stephanie fumbled in her handbag for her key, and suddenly she felt a rough hand on her wrist. She looked up into the face of Leon Ainsworth!

"Leon! What?! . . ."

"Go ahead, let us into your place, Stephanie."

She gripped the key tighter in her hand.

"I'll help you," he said with a leer, as he wrenched the key from her palm. He unlocked her apartment and stood aside.

"After you, my dear. Let's go in and have a little chat."

Stephanie backed off. "Leon, it's over with us. Now come on, I don't want to have any trouble."

"Trouble? Who said anything about trouble?" He smiled his most winning smile, and Stephanie's fear subsided a little. "I just want to have a little talk with you, sweetheart," he continued. "Come to talk about a . . . business proposition. Aren't you glad to see old Leon?"

Stephanie grabbed the key from his hand and went on into the apartment with him following.

"Now Leon, you know it's over and done with," she said. "It has been for years. I don't want to bring up anything about the past—about us."

A thought came to her. "How did you find me, anyway?"

He sat down on the sofa. "I live in Memphis now," he said. "I've been here for about a year. Very comfortable, I might add."

"So you left St. Louis. Why?"

"I ought to be the one asking the questions," he said. "But so you can see there's no malice, I'll answer yours. You see, my wife . . ."

"Your wife? You're married?"

"Sure, why not? And a very pretty thing she is too. Name's Helen." He closed his eyes in a gesture of smug self-satisfaction. "Well, her business brought us to Memphis."

Stephanie let out a sigh. "So you married her for her money, is that it?"

"You wrong me, Stephanie. She didn't have any money. Her father . . . well, it's a long story."

"Come on, out with it."

"Well, her father owned a business here, and he offered me a position in it. It turns out that his business wasn't on a very firm footing, and he folded, but I was able to squirrel away some money. I have a fairly good job now, and just the other day I saw you driving down the street. I followed you here. I didn't know what apartment you had, or I would have called on you yesterday."

Stephanie was standing in front of him, and he took her wrist. He looked into her eyes. Compared to Max, she thought, he looks like a cadaver.

"I have an offer to make, sweetheart."

"Don't you call me sweetheart! I'm not your sweetheart."

"Just listen. Now you know I've always been in love with you."

"Humph!"

"Come on and sit down," he said in a loud voice. He pulled her down onto the sofa beside him.

"The trouble is, I'm married now," he continued in a calmer tone. He had her arm in a viselike grip, and he put his other arm over her shoulders.

"Good. That means you'll let me alone."

"No it doesn't. Why Stephanie, I can't sleep for thinking about you." He was playing with the collar of her blouse.

"Well, it's no good, Leon." She tried to pull out of his grasp, but he just tightened his hold on her.

"And that's why I want to make you an offer."

"An offer?"

"Yes, it's like a . . . business proposal, sort of. I think it would be nice if you would—well, let me visit you here every once in a while. We could become lovers. You still fancy me, don't you?"

"Now Leon . . ."

"Maybe every other day, how does that sound?" He was still holding her tightly. "You know," he said, "I could make things pretty difficult for you. I know where you work . . ."

Stephanie was furious. With her free hand she landed a resounding slap on his face as hard as she could.

"Why you little bitch!" Leon grabbed both her arms and threw her onto the sofa. She went at him with her nails, but he lunged at her and pinned her arms.

"Oh, God!" she screamed. "Leon, leave me alone!" She was on the point of hysteria, but then with an effort of will she collected her wits.

"Wait, Leon! Wait," she said. "Maybe it's a good idea." She closed her eyes.

Leon hadn't expected her to acquiesce so easily. He relaxed his hold on her. Still he regarded her with suspicion.

Summoning her womanly strength, she smiled at him with half-closed eyelids. "In fact," she said, "it might be nice. I don't have any attachments now, nothing like a steady."

"I knew you'd see it my way," he said. With a smile on his face he looked at the bedroom door. "Then what do you say to . . . tomorrow? My lunch hour's almost over now, but I get off at five, and I could be here sometime after that—say five thirty."

He was moving toward the door. "Wait a minute," he said. "Let's seal this with a kiss."

He walked back to the sofa where Stephanie was sitting and bent down. She kissed him lightly on the lips.

"Come on, Stephanie. You can do better than that!"

"Oh, Leon, I'm not feeling too well right now."

"Well, all right," he said, and was gone. And when he was gone she gave way to her tears. She had come through a lot, and up to now she could thrust and parry. The situation at the office wasn't comforting, but compared to this it was nothing.

It was volatile at the mill, though, especially in regard to Max. With him she had to tread lightly. She had already offended him, through no fault of her own, and it was impossible to tell what he really thought about her relationship with Terry Sells.

Max was as effusive as a clam when it came to venting his own feelings. He hadn't said anything about Terry except for the information that Terry collects collectibles. But Max certainly had brooded.

And what would Max say about this horrid situation she had gotten herself into with Leon? Up to now he had no knowledge of Leon or of her relationship with him. He only knew that she had "a past," but he was going to find out about Leon now.

She dialed Max's office number. Jennifer, the receptionist, answered with a cheery "good afternoon."

"Max, please. It's Stephanie."

"Max, I'm sorry to bother you, but I have to see you," she said when he came on the telephone. "If it's not too much trouble, would you mind stopping by here after work?"

"No trouble at all," he said. He could tell from her voice that something was upsetting her. And he wasn't one to smolder over a tiff like the one he had had with her that morning. "I'll leave here around four thirty."

He arrived at her apartment a few minutes before five. The redness was gone out of Stephanie's eyes, but her voice was still slightly shaky. She had spent the last few hours between dozing and thinking about Leon's "proposition," and about Max and what she would say to him.

Max sat on the sofa. Stephanie offered him tea, and as she poured it she stole a glance at him. He was obviously puzzled about why she had called him. But his face still gave Stephanie the feeling that he was self-confident, that there was no problem too large for him to solve. And the nobility of his features made her heart flutter. She handed him his tea and sat beside him on the sofa.

"Max, I want to tell you about Leon," she said.

Seven

Leon

Stephanie's living room was not large, but it was beautifully and elegantly furnished. Sitting on the deep blue sofa with his teacup, Max reminded Stephanie of an illustration in a gentleman's magazine. The dark wood of the butler's table in front of the sofa reflected the subdued light in the room, and Max's lively eyes caught that light. He looked at her with a question.

"Leon?"

"Leon Ainsworth."

"Now Stephanie, I told you I didn't want to hear about your past. It's enough for me to know that you have a past of some sort. It doesn't bother me. I say let's forget it."

"It's not the past any more, it's the present. And I have to tell you. You'll see—just hear me out."

She told him about her engagement. Leon had been charming to her, and she had become infatuated with him. He was working as a shipping clerk in her father's business, and she was doing secretarial and receptionist duties.

"I was twenty when he proposed to me. I thought it was the beginning of a great romance, of a story come true. You can't imagine how I felt. I had everything to look forward to—children, a secure future. I would be the mistress of a large household, with a husband who loved me—

"I didn't think about whether I loved him or not. If I had I suppose I would have found out then—but that came later. I certainly was caught up with the idea of marriage, though. We set a date.

"My father was a vice president at Triangle Cartons, and of course I had the run of the plant. One day I was down in the stockroom looking for some office supplies, when I heard the outer door open. The little room in which the supplies were kept was closed off from the main shelf area of the stockroom by a swinging door. So I couldn't see who came into the stockroom, but I heard Leon's voice.

"He was talking to somebody on the stock crew. 'What about that chick up front, Stephanie?' said the man. 'You're pretty thick with her, aren't you?'

"'Thick with her?' said Leon. 'You damn right I am. I'm gonna marry her.'

"'You are? It's a case of true love, I guess,' said the other man.

"'Don't be silly,' said Leon. 'Don't you know, she's the boss's daughter. Old man Gray. Haven't you seen that movie where the guy marries the company president's daughter? It's instant riches for him. And he has all the women he wants on the side.'

"By this time I was really feeling rotten, Max. I wanted to burst in on them, but I just couldn't do it. I kept quiet, even though I felt like an eavesdropper. I could hardly believe they were talking about me." She put her hand on Max's arm.

"'But you do love her, don't you?' asked the other man.

"'Oh, Hell, I don't know,' said Leon. 'Oh, she's pretty enough, but no, she's going to be my ticket to a long . . . association with this company. And besides that, I already have Helen.'

"And they went out talking, Max, talking and laughing. Laughing about how gullible I was, and how Leon was going to use me to move up in the business."

Max was clenching his jaw. He was speechless with rage.

"I don't have to tell you that was the end of our engagement. My eyes were opened, and strangely enough, I didn't feel like I thought I should feel, because I came to the realization that I had never loved him at all. I was simply infatuated with him—with him and with the idea of marriage.

"That's when I left Triangle and went to Chariton Products. I just couldn't stay on and face some of those people. I don't know how many people he told about his scheme, but I couldn't face any of them. My father was a bulwark of strength at the time."

"So you did tell him," put in Max.

"Yes, and he dealt with Leon, how harshly I don't know. Leon didn't last at Triangle, I do know that."

Incredulity was registered on Max's face.

"I called you, Max, because I'm at my wit's end. Leon was here today at noon."

"He was? What nerve! I hope you sent him packing, preferably with a swift kick to the seat of the pants—just what cur like him would deserve."

"Oh, but Max, that's not all. He's asked me to—be his mistress. He's married, and he wants me on the side."

"Good God! What did you do?"

"There wasn't much I could do, Max. He's too strong for me to fight him. And he's coming here tomorrow."

"Didn't you tell him to get lost?"

"He's brutal, Max. He would have forced me. In fact he had me pinned on the sofa here, and I didn't have any choice but to tell him it was all right." She bit her lip, and put her head on Max's shoulder.

"Don't worry, Stephanie." Max kissed her hair. "We'll just get a restraining order against him. What time is he coming?"

"Five thirty. Oh, Max, I didn't know what to do. That's why I called you." Her eyes were damp and she touched his cheek with her lips.

"Don't worry, we'll take care of him," he said.

She nestled in his arms, and he kissed her tenderly. "You don't have anything to feel uncomfortable about," he said. "In the meantime, aren't you getting hungry? We can go for something to eat."

"Can we go to that same little cafe you took me to the first night I came to Memphis? It would be perfect to lift my spirits. After all, this has been a rotten day for me."

"I know it has, and I apologize for acting so . . . cold to you at the office. Terry Sells is harmless, and I shouldn't have gotten so jealous of him, but . . . well, I . . ."

"You what?" Stephanie glanced at him, but he had turned his face away.

"Oh, it's nothing. Well, how about dinner now?" He had obviously wanted to say something to her but broke off, feeling she had been through enough for one day.

The next day Stephanie had lunch with Lorraine Pringle in the plant cafeteria. "Something's bothering you, Stephanie, I can tell," said Lorraine over her salad plate. "Or shouldn't I ask?"

Lorraine had become almost like a mother-image to Stephanie. She was considerate and helpful, and she seemed to know just when to leave Stephanie to her own thoughts.

"Sure you can ask, Lorraine. I've just been having some personal problems. You see, the man I was engaged to a long time ago has shown up here in Memphis, and he's pestering me. I'm just upset about that, but Max has promised to help me, and I think everything will work out all right. Thanks for asking." She patted Lorraine's arm.

Lorraine looked at her with almost a conspiratorial look. "I'll tell you something, Stephanie," she said. "Mr. Lamartine—Max—is quite a person to have on your side. He always seems to know what to do in a difficult situation. You'll find that he's always willing to help, and he doesn't expect anything in return. I'm glad you two hit it off so well together."

"Well, maybe we haven't."

"Oh, you mean because of Terry." Lorraine laughed. "Stephanie, you know, I can see right through you. You were never serious about Terry—not after one date, anyway, and I'll tell you something else. You'd never be serious about him, if you had a hundred dates with him. You know why?"

"I have an idea, but—"

"Because Terry, as nice a fellow as he is, is sort of like an evangelist. He's very nice to everybody, but that's where it stops. He'll never be any closer to you than he was the other day, no matter how long you know him."

"But he's so outgoing and friendly. I liked him right away when I first met him."

"Everybody does. Terry is a very likeable guy. But Stephanie, just between you and me, I think he's essentially a lonely man."

"Why?"

"Because everything about his personality—

his friendliness, his outgoing nature, his way of smiling—all those things are learned. Now this is all my own opinion. You see, he took a success course, the same course a lot of businessmen take, and instead of using the methods to enhance his personality, he emphasized the methods so much that he let them supplant his personality—sort of take over. That's why I think he doesn't have any real close friends. And I don't mean to sound like I don't like him, because I do. But don't look for anything deep in the man, it's just not there."

"Are you giving me advice?"

"You mean, should you go out with him again? Well, not really advice. As I said, he's a very likeable man. But you'll have to decide for yourself if he asks you again."

What an interesting conversation, Stephanie thought when she went back to her office after lunch. She realized that Lorraine was right about Terry. It explained about the things she had observed in his character on Saturday. He was a likeable guy, as Lorraine had said, and Stephanie decided to simply take him at face value.

She hadn't seen him all day, so she went down to his office. They exchanged greetings, but he was busy, and Stephanie went back to her office. By four thirty she had almost cleared her desk of the tax information she was working on, and only had one letter left to type for the day. About that time Max strode in.

"I hope you don't have anything that can't wait until tomorrow," he said.

"I was just going to type this letter to Mr. Springer in Stanley."

"That can wait. I think we ought to go to your apartment now, just in case this Leon character decides to come early. It certainly wouldn't do for him to get there before we do."

"Oh, you're coming with me?"

"Well, of course I am. I think it's best."

She drove home with Max following. She had been dreading going home all day, but now that Max was with her she didn't worry.

Just after they shut the door there was a ring at the doorbell. "It's not five yet," she said.

"Max went to the door. "Come in," he said. A rather short man in a business suit entered.

"Stephanie, this is Sergeant Bill Mulvane, of the Memphis police."

"I have this injunction for you to sign, Miss Gray," said Sergeant Mulvane. "Both copies."

She glanced over the papers and signed them. "This is not the way we usually do it," said the policeman, "but Max said this was an unusual situation." He smiled at Stephanie.

"When the man comes, you just let him in as if you were glad to see him," he continued. "You don't have to pretend you are, you understand, but just don't let him suspect anything out of the ordinary. Close the door as soon as he comes in, but don't say anything after you do. Max and I will be over here." He went over to stand with Max behind the door in such a manner as to be shielded by the door when it was open.

Sergeant Mulvane had hardly finished speaking when the door-bell rang. He winked at Stephanie as she went to the door.

"Hello, sweetheart," said Leon as he stepped into the room. She shut the door. "What?! Who are these men?"

Sergeant Mulvane had his wallet out to show his identification. "Memphis PD," he said. "Stay right where you are, Mr. Ainsworth," he continued, as Leon half turned toward the door. He had a surprised look on his face, and he looked questioningly at Stephanie.

Stephanie didn't venture a word.

"Now look here," said Leon, "you don't have anything on me. I have rights, you know." He was looking from Sergeant Mulvane to Max and back again.

"Oh, I know that," said the policeman. "I can read your rights to you, if it comes to that."

Leon glanced at Stephanie. "This woman invited me here . . ."

"Oh, did she?" said Sergeant Mulvane. "Tell me more. What was the purpose of her invitation?"

"Well," said Leon with a swaggering expression, "she's in love with me."

Max laughed, and Stephanie joined in his laughter.

"What's the opinion of Mrs. Ainsworth on that subject?" asked Sergeant Mulvane. "Shall we call Helen Ainsworth to find out?"

Leon spluttered. "Now see here, there's nothing illegal about me seeing this woman!" He looked at Stephanie, whose expression couldn't be read.

"Calm down, Ainsworth. Otherwise I'll have to take you down to the station and book you."

"On what charge?" He was still swaggering.

"How about attempted rape, for starters? Or illegal entry, or . . . looking back at your record, I think we can probably get you for extortion."

Leon hung his head. Then he looked at Stephanie. "Stephanie . . ." he began. Her lips were set, and she shook her head. It was obvious that she wouldn't help him.

"Okay, okay," he said to Sergeant Mulvane. "Let's get it over with."

"Miss Gray isn't pressing charges for attempted rape, Mr. Ainsworth, and I think you're lucky. But we have our eye on you."

"Am I free to go, then?"

"Not until I've given you this. It's simply a restraining order, and you'll notice Miss Gray's signature on it. It says you are not to be found anywhere near this apartment unit, or anywhere near Miss Stephanie Gray. If you are, we'll book you so fast your head will swim. And I'll tell you something. I'll look back over your record myself, and we'll find plenty to keep you in the cage for a long time. Is that clear?"

Leon just nodded his head and took the paper.

"Then vamoose, pal. And make it quick before I change my mind."

Stephanie sighed when Leon left. "I can't tell you how much I appreciate what you did, Sergeant."

"Just doing my job," he replied. "I'm not really as mean as that, but I have to get tough with some of these characters." He smiled at Stephanie. "I don't believe you'll have any more trouble with him. If you do, just call the department and ask for me."

"Won't you stay for coffee?"

"I have to run, but thanks anyway."

Max shook his hand. "Thanks again, Bill. I don't think we'll have a repeat of that, do you?"

"I sure hope not." He smiled at Stephanie again, and was gone.

When he left, Stephanie went over to where Max was standing. "I can't help it," she said, as a tear rolled down her cheek. "That was just a traumatic experience for me."

He took her in his arms. She was convinced that somehow he was feeling everything she was. Then she realized that she was spending a lot of time with his arms around her, and that she was enjoying it immensely. She felt this was where she belonged, in Max's arms.

"Right now I have some legal problems of my own to take care of," said Max, "with Neils Patterson. But it isn't as upsetting as what we just went through. It's important, though, or I'd call it off and we could go out together."

"I just feel drained, Max. I don't think I'd be very good company."

"What about tomorrow, then?" he said. The Music Circle is sponsoring a fine pianist. Do you enjoy classical music?"

"Yes, I do." She was wide-eyed. "But I didn't know you did."

"He's playing three Beethoven sonatas, including the 'Waldstein.' I'd be pleased if you would go with me."

"I'd love it, Max." She hadn't heard anything like an excellent pianist since she left St. Louis, but she had been afraid that Max wasn't a music lover.

"Let's say six, then? We'll go for dinner, and then to the auditorium."

Stephanie took off from work early the next day. Max represented an authority figure to her, a very dominant personality. But why did she let his personality affect her so?

Her anticipation for the evening was such that she found it difficult to concentrate on what she would wear. She chose a powder blue A-line dress with long sleeves and a bolero-type jacket. She wanted to dress simply but appealingly. She parted her hair on the side and swept the front across her forehead.

So much had happened to her in less than a week since she had been in Memphis. She felt that Max was becoming a dominant figure in her life, much more than just a friend or even employer. Always when he looks at me with those beautiful eyes, she thought, I can't seem to control my emotions.

Well, I won't let him take charge of me as he undoubtedly takes charge of everyone else. It's obvious that Lorraine idolizes him, and I'm sure everyone else at the plant does too. But I can't let him control me like Leon did. I told Grandmother that he inherited his business, but I'm not really sure. It might be that he acquired it the same way his uncle acquired his riches. Marla O'Neal said to be careful about him, and more than once I've had a sixth sense that he is dangerous. But then why do I compromise my better judgment and go with him?

But she couldn't answer her own question. Instead she found herself trying to look as attractive as she could for him, in anticipation of their date.

Max was dressed in a navy pin-stripe suit with a maroon knit tie. They went to a cozy restaurant for an unhurried dinner. Max talked about Beethoven and about the piano—he played, but he admitted that he wasn't entitled to call himself a "pianist." For dinner they had fowl, with a light Rhine wine. A perfect meal to precede an evening of music.

The pianist played superbly. He was a small wiry man with a huge shock of coal black hair and long fingers. He looked the way Stephanie imagined Franz Liszt must have looked as a piano virtuoso. And his playing was equally diabolic, as if Satan himself were guiding his fingers on the keys.

She loved the 'Waldstein,' but she was transported into another world when he played the slow movement of the 'Pathétique.'

Stephanie looked over at Max during that movement. He was absorbed in the sound, and as she traced his silhouette in the semi-darkness, her skin tingled and she felt that now familiar urge to nestle in his arms, that desire that seemed to envelope her when she thought about how he had held her and kissed her before. He turned his head slightly to look at her, and though he didn't utter a sound, she felt as if he were asking a question of her, to which she could only say <u>yes</u>. It was only a single glance, but it took hold of her like a strong wind, insistent, almost savage, and at the same time refreshing, filling her soul until she felt she would burst.

She felt Max's hand grasp hers, and the contact sent a wave of recognition through her body. If he can do that to me with a simple touch, she thought, how much more can he do when he enfolds me with those strong arms. "Be careful," Marla warned—this is what she was warning me against.

"Would you like to stop by my house for a nightcap?" he asked as they left the auditorium. "It's right on the way. I know you have to be at work early in the morning," he said with a grin, "but I promise to let you get home in time for a good night's sleep."

"Well, if you put it that way, I suppose I can't refuse."

It was only a short drive from town, and he pulled his car up in front of the large house. The driveway curved around, leading up to the front door. It was an old house of the kind that was built by the leading Memphis families before the Second World War, one of the huge showplaces of Memphis.

"Rich in associations, I imagine," said Stephanie, half to herself.

Max cocked his head. "You're right. This home has been in the Lamartine family for generations."

As he opened the door Stephanie was met by a sight right out of an ante-bellum Southern novel. The lights were on low—Max explained that the day servants left them on when they went home. He led her through a spacious foyer into a huge sunken living room. He invited her to sit on the long couch and went over to a small bar in the corner of the room to pour a glass of brandy for himself and one for Stephanie.

She tasted the aromatic liquid and set the snifter down on the glass-top coffee table. He sat near her and she turned to look into his eyes. In them she saw that same question, that same urgency she had perceived at the recital. And she felt herself surrendering as he drew her to him.

"I need you, Stephanie," he said in a husky whisper as his lips found hers. She knew she should resist him, but she was unable to pull away from him of her own will. The kiss was probing, urgent, yet tender at the same time. She felt his fingers tracing sensuous lines on the skin of her neck, and it increased her desire.

"Oh, Max," she breathed, "there are too many questions—I need more time, I need to know more." She made a feeble attempt to push him away, but her desire was mounting, and she only kissed him more fervently.

Her dress was buttoned on either shoulder, and he unbuttoned the three buttons on her right shoulder, one at a time. Then he undid the buttons on her left shoulder, and she helped him unfasten the front closure of her bra.

He touched the sensitive skin of her chest with his lips and tongue, and slowly, maddeningly found his way down to her breasts, evoking a response in her that moved her closer against his body. With his fingers still moving sensuously on her skin he half rose, and she rose with him. Removing his tie, he undid his shirt and slid out of it, while she slipped out of her dress.

She ran her hand across his broad chest, and she knew the questions that had come to her mind were unimportant in the interval of this sensuous moment. She gave herself up to him, and he very gently found the warm seat of her desire with his fingertips, at the same time loosening his clothing.

"Stephanie, I want you so badly. You drive me wild," he said as his tongue lightly brushed her skin sensuously. "I want to make love to you. Tell me you want me."

"Max, Max, yes, I want you. I need you," she responded.

Something deep within her was saying "dangerous," but another part of her was crying out for fulfillment.

Then she was surrendering her body to him and she felt his warmth, still and quiet at first, then with a mounting tension, bringing her to the peak of ecstasy, gliding with this half savage, half tender man to the height of passion.

How long she slept Stephanie couldn't tell. She only knew that Max had carried her into a bedroom and covered her with a light cloth, and that she had been clinging to him for what seemed like hours. She opened her eyes and saw that he had turned off all but a dim light. He was looking at her when she woke, and he kissed her eyes.

A smile came to her lips. He looked so familiar, like a graven image of the man she had dreamed of as a child, dreamed of in her teens, and here he was lying beside her, and she was looking at him through half-closed eyes.

Images formed in her mind, images of Max appearing from nowhere to seize Jerry Osgood and to take her into his arms, and she remembered in exquisite detail how she thrilled to his touch. Again she conjured up the image of him seated at his desk beside her at Carmichael's house, and of him taking her into his arms there. And her mind wandered to the airplane trip to New Orleans, and she could almost feel the softness of his lips as he spoke of beauty and of the setting sun.

Suddenly Stephanie looked around her. "Max, it's late," she said. "I don't know how long I slept. But I have to get home. And . . . my clothes."

"Relax, beautiful woman. In the first place, it's not late—it's not even one o'clock. You wouldn't call that late, would you?"

"Sure I would. You would too, if you worked for a man who was a brutal savage. He might chew me up and feed me to the lions if I'm late."

"He sure will," said Max, and rolled over to pin her arms and to rain a multitude of kisses on her face, neck, and throat.

"Your clothes are on the chair there by the bed," he went on. "But you don't want to clothe that beautiful body, to hide it from my eyes, do you?"

"That's not the question," she replied. "It's only a question of propriety."

"Propriety be damned!"

"I feel the same way, Max." she touched his cheek with her hand, and kissed the corner of his mouth. "But it's just too late and I have to go."

She slipped her clothes on and the walked together, arm in arm, through the silent house to his car. When he let her into her apartment, she removed her clothes and fell into the bed almost straightway into the arms of profound slumber.

Morning came early, all too early for Stephanie. She decided to take her time about going in to the office, and to have a leisurely breakfast.

Over her breakfast she went over the events of the previous evening in her mind. On the one hand, a wonderful evening. Certainly she was attracted to Max. God, how she was attracted to Max! But so many things had happened to her so quickly that she was utterly confused about what it all meant. She found herself staring into her coffee cup almost expecting to find the answers there. But the answers didn't come.

What did it all mean? There was Terry Sells, squeaky clean—antiseptic. And there was Max. There was Lorraine Pringle, talking to her about Terry, and—about Max. There was Marla O'Neal—and there was Max. Everything that came to her mind seemed to end finally in the image of Max.

A sudden tremor shook her body, and she dropped the teaspoon from her hand. She was in love with him! She had never felt this way toward a man. She told herself it was emotional, but it seemed to be physical—it certainly culminated in a physical need. It also did strange things to her physically. Made her spine tingle, made her blush, made her cry. There was no doubt, it had a physical manifestation.

She stood up and went to the kitchen to refill her coffee cup. On the way she stopped at the long mirror that hung on the wall in the dining area. Her first reaction was shock—she hadn't even thought about how she looked this morning. She was unable to think of anything but Max. Running her fingers through her hair, she thought: how unreal this whole dream is. Maximilian Lamartine is the Chairman of the Board of a huge conglomerate. He is the nephew of a man who was viler than the vilest dregs of humanity. He was probably involved in just as many illegal schemes as his uncle had been. That was the thing she couldn't condone. And he probably had a different woman in that same bed every night. There was no doubt about it; she had been right before when she had assumed that he was a practiced lover.

But regardless of all those objections, she loved him. And looking back, she realized she had loved him all along, from that first day when he helped her out on the highway. What a fool she had been not to recognize it.

But no matter how she rationalized it, she knew it was impossible that he could feel the same way about her. It was just too far-fetched. She went over and over it in her mind, after that initial feeling of exhilaration, and she always came up with the same answer: Max Lamartine was an important man, too important to get himself mixed up with a woman in the way their relationship was heading. Even if Stephanie had been an important woman in her own right. Oh, she was important. She knew she had a grand destiny of some sort. But her importance was only to herself, not in the eyes of the world. And it was the world that judged Maximilian Lamartine.

By nine thirty Stephanie had gotten dressed, principally in order to combat despair and confusion. She reasoned that she would feel better with a bath and spiffy clothes. And it helped. But still she was faced with a dead end. First a joyous realization that she actually was in love, in love with the man who was everything she had ever dreamed of—with the only man she could ever love.

But then she was faced with the devastating surety that she couldn't do anything about it. Max was his own man, and no matter what happened between them, she would still always go home alone.

It was in this confusing state of mind that she went to the office. The work seemed to have piled up on her desk overnight. Max wasn't in, and Lorraine was busy every minute. Even Terry didn't have time to talk to her.

Finally at lunch time she went in to Lorraine.

"Lorraine, what's going on? I need to consult Max about something, and I haven't seen him all morning." She didn't really have any idea what she would say to Max if he had been there.

"I'm sorry Stephanie, I can't talk right now, I have a lunch date with a buyer. Mr. Lamartine won't be in again today. I'll talk to you later."

So Stephanie had lunch with Jennifer, who was perfectly suited for her job as receptionist, with her gift for conversation. In fact Jennifer talked about her little boy Robby all during lunch. Robby was in a nursery school, and Stephanie had seen him once. She loved little children, especially four-year-olds, and Robby seemed to have been made after the model of angels—that is, in the cuteness department. So it was no wonder Jennifer talked about him almost non-stop.

Max's habit was to leave the work for Stephanie on her desk in a letter tray, and any work beyond that he would discuss with her personally.

She had a few letters to write and some of the bills to mark for payment, plus some work on titles, and then she would be caught up. She figured she would be through by Friday afternoon late. She went back to her desk, hoping Lorraine would stop in after her lunch. But by four o'clock Lorraine hadn't come back, and she asked Marianne, one of the stenographers, where Lorraine was.

"Lorraine gave me a buzz a while ago," replied Marianne. "She said she wouldn't be back in today, and to take her calls. The truth is, she hasn't gotten any yet," she added.

"Where is Mr. Lamartine?" asked Stephanie, keenly aware of his name and how it sounded coming from her mouth, like a new sensation.

"I'm not really sure where he went, but Lorraine said he would probably be gone the rest of the day."

Stephanie worked a little while longer, and then closed her desk and went home. She did a little cleaning around the apartment and did her laundry in the apartment co-op. Then she went across the street for a fast-food supper.

Now she knew why she had that empty feeling—she had experienced it off and on for some months. It was because she was in love with Max, and whenever he wasn't with her she felt that way—empty, unfulfilled.

Back at her apartment she undressed and put on a robe. Then she brewed a cup of tea. The walls seemed to hold a likeness of Max. She could almost hear his voice; almost feel his hands as they touched her, awakening her passion. No, she shouldn't have let him make love to her last night. It was only an invitation for more, and where would it lead—where could it lead? To a broken heart, nothing more. To a few fleeting moments of passion—she couldn't deny that she desired him—but that was it. And in the end, she would go home, go back to Stanley, back to St. Louis perhaps, alone.

Suddenly the doorbell rang. Stephanie looked at the clock with a certain fear clutching at her. It was late. It could even be Leon again. But surely he wouldn't come back, not after Sergeant Mulvane served him that restraining order. To see who it was she had to open the door.

It rang again, this time accompanied by a light knock. Stephanie opened the door. Max.

"I was hoping you'd be home," he said. "I had to see you."

He came to her and placed his hands on her waist. She buried her head in his neck and shivered with excitement. She didn't want him to see how glad she was that he came, but she couldn't restrain her feelings.

Then she backed off from him. "I'm just having a cup of tea. Would you like some?" she asked as she walked toward the kitchen, trying to avoid his eyes.

"Yes, I think that would be nice."

"Well, Max," she said nonchalantly, "I missed you at the office." She handed him his tea.

I had to be in Burlington this afternoon. I just got back."

"Oh, have you had dinner? I can fix something for you . . ."

"No, I've eaten."

She sat on the blue couch beside him. Each took a sip of tea.

"Stephanie, I have to talk to you," he said. "I have to straighten out some things about us, about our personal relationship." He looked exceedingly handsome in the soft light of her living room, with his silk shirt open at the collar, where he had removed his tie.

"Forgive me for sounding so businesslike," he added.

Here it comes, she thought to herself. Almost the identical proposition Leon had made.

She put her finger on his lips. "Don't," she said. "Let's just enjoy each other's company for a while."

She knew she looked seductive in her velour robe. She had nothing on under her robe, and her skin tingled as he put his hand on her neck to gently pull her over to him. What a fascination this man has over me, she thought. But he wants to make a business deal with me just like Leon wanted to do. Why didn't I see it?

She gave way to the irresistible urge to feel his bare chest under his silk shirt, and as she glided her hand across his chest, inhaling his musky tang, he pulled her closer and erotically nibbled her earlobe, then showered kisses down her neck and delicately kissed the sensitive skin of her breasts.

"Stephanie, I told you that you drive me wild. Last night wasn't enough for me, you know that. And I told you before, I get what I want."

Somewhere in the dim recesses of her mind she thought he was being arrogant, but her body was succumbing to his sensuous play. She couldn't resist him now if she had wanted to. She undid his shirt buttons and slid her hands into find his muscular chest and back. His palm moved down from the flat of her stomach to gently and teasingly touch the most sensitive parts of her body and thighs.

"Max," she groaned between half-open lips. Business proposals be damned, she had to have this man. All her caution was flung to the wind.

He stood up from the couch, and led her by the hand into her bedroom. He put one knee on the bed and eased her onto her back, playfully undoing the belt that held her robe closed. She grasped the open front of his shirt with both hands and pulled him down onto her. Her desire was growing, and it made him more eager than ever to satisfy his own.

In an instant he was out of his shirt, and she marveled at his bronzed muscles as he encircled her body with his arms.

"Do you want me?" he asked.

"Oh, God, yes, Max."

"How much?" he whispered. "Enough to take me to you every night?"

She would promise him anything. "Yes, Max, anything you ask."

"I told you I get what I want," he said as he explored her shoulders and breasts with his mouth. "But I wouldn't take you against your will."

His trousers had slid to the floor, and he lay up against her body, his taught muscles forming a contrast to her soft and delicate skin. Then with an easy motion he came to her as his lips and tongue found her mouth. He began gently and quietly, promising the fulfillment of her crying need.

He whispered to her, "Last night I realized that I had to have you at any risk. Leon, Marv, Terry—is there no one else?"

"No one, Max. There couldn't be anyone."

"And there won't be anyone else, will you promise me that?"

No one," she repeated. "Max, I need you," she cried in her passion. Stephanie was rendered almost senseless as Max took her to the height of their mutual passion, more satisfying, more fulfilling even than the previous night. Then she lay quietly in his arms for a long time, unable to move, almost crying with the joy of the aftermath of their love-making.

By the light from the kitchen she could see him lying prone beside her, his dark hair curling round his ears—touched with gray—with his eyes closed. Again she realized that he was the man she had dreamed about, and that she had longed for him to take her in his arms. And now he had taken her in his arms and whispered words of love to her, and she had given herself to him and everything was right.

But she was plagued by a problem, growing more insistent with every breath she took. Everything was right, except that this wasn't a story book; he wasn't a romantic hero, like the golden king ("crown and sceptre and everything") who would take her off with him to some great castle on top of a glass mountain.

This was the twenty first century, and Max— this very man lying beside her in his beauty—was very much a man of the twenty first century, not likely to fit into the mold of the medieval hero, not likely to pay the slightest attention to the needs or desires of a woman like Stephanie.

But the undeniable truth kept ringing in her ears: I love this man! I'm willing to sacrifice everything for him but my principles. And that's what he wants me to do—to become his mistress, just like Leon wanted. If he knew how much I love him, he could get what he wanted, because I simply can't resist him. But as long as he doesn't know my weakness, he won't be able to "bargain" with me for "love at convenience."

He opened his eyes. She nestled against his shoulder, and he ran his fingers through her hair.

Time stood still, and she closed her eyes, only to open them in surprise some minutes later. She had slept, and Max was standing by the bed with a glass of cream sherry in either hand.

"Thanks." She looked at him over the rim of the glass and sipped the wine. He had slipped on his clothes, and now he sat on the bed by her side.

"Do you usually greet people at the door with nothing on but a robe?" he asked.

She blushed slightly. "No, but I was getting ready for bed."

"You said you don't have a lover," he said. "You said you won't have another man. I want to be your only lover. You'll promise me that?"

This was the contract. She couldn't show her hand, it would bind her to him. This isn't what she wanted. Oh, she wanted Max—God, how she wanted him. But not like that. Not for him to come to her when he had a sexual craving—at his own convenience. And who knows who he would go to the next night.

She laughed derisively. "To be my only lover? This isn't love, this is sex."

He was silent. His face assumed that impenetrable mask by degrees. After a moment he asked quietly, "Tell me, Stephanie, do you love me?"

To keep from crying she flung it at him: "No! And I won't be your mistress, or your slut!"

Now his face showed his hurt and bewilderment, and she was suddenly confused. She put her hands up to her face. She couldn't afford to cry now. After a minute she felt him stroke her hair silently. She backed up against the headboard, turning her face away from him. There seemed to be nothing more to say, but inside she was crying. She had hurt him—hurt him deeply, and she had hurt herself, but she couldn't take it back—her pride wouldn't let her.

"I'll go, then," he said. "I can find my own way out. Go on to sleep." He gathered his shirt up and slipped it on. As he tucked in the tail of the shirt, he looked at her. "By the way, our work with the estate will be done after tomorrow. I won't need you after that."

And he was gone. Stephanie was stunned, too stunned to even think of what she should have said, or if there was anything else she <u>could</u> have said. The only man she could have ever loved, and as he walked out her door she knew he was walking out of her life. Was she rationalizing when she told herself that he was just like Carmichael, and that, just like Leon, he would have had her only on his own terms, and that when he was through with her he would literally throw her away, a broken woman?

She cried, and slept. Off and on through the night she woke to look over at the pillow beside her where he had lain, and a flood of confused emotions shook her body.

She went in early the next morning. Her eyes were red, and Lorraine noticed them. She was immediately concerned.

"What's the problem, Stephanie? Have you been crying?"

"Oh, no," she lied. "I think I've just caught a cold. It's nothing." She shut the door to her office and worked furiously. Max had said he wouldn't need her after today—well, that was fine! He was the only person she could ever love, and now she didn't have a chance. He could never return her love, anyway. He simply wanted her to use, to gratify his sexual appetite—and he had quite a sexual appetite.

Still she had to venture a peek into his office on her way out. Lorraine had left her desk for a moment, and she opened the door to his office. His office was dark.

Lorraine came up, and Stephanie turned around. "Are you looking for Max?" asked Lorraine.

"Well, yes."

"He's gone out of town. I don't know when he'll be back."

"Lorraine, I'll be going too," said Stephanie. "I won't be back, since I've finished the work on the estate."

"Oh. Well, it's been delightful knowing you, Stephanie. Keep in touch with us, will you? Let us hear from you once in a while. I know you'll be talking to Max every now and then."

Stephanie noticed a pixie look on Lorraine's face, and tried to ignore it. "Thank you, Lorraine. Tell Terry goodbye for me, too." She forced a smile and waved her hand as she went down the hall rather in a hurry.

Stephanie couldn't bear to be in the apartment for long. Before she took the key to the apartment office, she took a last glance around, her eyes dwelling only for a moment on the blue sofa.

Eight

Decisions

Stephanie's car purred along, anxious to shorten the miles between Memphis and Stanley. Fall was rapidly approaching, and there was a little nip in the air. It was still short-sleeve weather, though, and Stephanie was dressed simply and comfortably in a cotton blouse and jeans. The fields were still green, but here and there she could see brown patches waiting to be ploughed for fall planting.

Her grandmother would be surprised that she was back so soon. So would Betsy. She tried to think about them, and about Nola, to keep from thinking about Max.

Max! The very name conjured up all sorts of images to her mind. She could feel his hand touching her face, hear his voice as he said her name. She shuddered as she thought about his dark eyes boring into hers, promising her so much. And then the bliss she had experienced in his arms—it had taken her to another world, to the peak of physical and emotional fulfillment.

That was then. This is now. Reluctantly, she forced herself to think of other things. Leon. Leon had shown his true colors. How could she ever have been enamored of him, of all people? But he had been put in his place at last—probably the first time anyone has ever seen through him, except of course his wife.

Stephanie felt sorry for her—Helen was her name, and by now she knew what a reprobate Leon was. Leon's fangs had been pulled by Sergeant Mulvane of the Memphis police. Stephanie smiled. By Sergeant Mulvane and Max. She could never forget how Max looked when Leon showed up. He had frightened Leon without saying a word.

Max again. Would she never be able to collect her thoughts again without him intruding upon them?

The trip to her grandmother's was just over three hours, and after the first hour and a half she stopped for gas. She pulled up to the full service pump to have her oil checked. A brisk, wiry little man serviced her car quickly. What a comical contrast to the man at the service station near Stanley, who moved and spoke so lethargically. That was when she first saw Max! It hadn't been very long ago, now that she thought about it, but it seemed as if she had known him forever.

That was in the past now, and she had to put it out of her mind. She had to completely divorce her thoughts from Max from now on, or she would never have any peace.

It was late in the afternoon when she finally pulled up into her grandmother's driveway. She hadn't turned off the motor when Betsy came running out.

"Stephanie! You're back soon. Your grandmother will be glad to see you." Betsy was genuinely happy to have her back, sweet girl that she was. And when she went in, her grandmother began to plan a big meal. That was her way to show affection, to show how glad she was to see Stephanie.

"How did it go in Memphis, Stephanie?" asked Mrs. Kimball. She noticed an expression of uncertainty that Stephanie couldn't conceal. "Is anything wrong?"

"No, Grandmother, it's just that I've had a long drive and I'm excited to be back, and . . . well, I'm a little tired."

"Why don't your stretch out there on the sofa, then? Or better yet, go on up to your room and take forty winks. Don't worry, we'll call you in time for dinner."

By the time Stephanie came down for dinner she felt more like her old self again. The talk flew over the dinner table. Stephanie told her grand-mother all about Memphis, about how large the city was, and about some of the malls and restaurants. Mrs. Kimball reminisced about how things had been in Memphis when she was a young woman—she had gone to Memphis frequently then. Judson took her there before they were married, took her dancing. She grew a little excited telling it.

"You wouldn't believe some of the streets were paved with red brick. They say there are still some brick streets in Memphis, even now. You may not have seen them—little side streets."

"I do remember seeing some of the little side streets, Grandmother. And—oh, I saw everything else, too. I loved that huge bridge over the Mississippi! Memphis is such a huge place now, and modern, too. I'll bet you wouldn't even recognize it."

"And how is Mr. Lamartine?"

"How is—oh, Max?" Against her will Stephanie blushed slightly.

Her grandmother pretended not to notice. "Yes, tell me about his company."

"There's not a lot to tell. It's a very huge mill, with hundreds of employees. I met several very nice people there. Have you ever seen the inside of a textile mill before?"

"I suppose not. Did he take you through?"

Stephanie nodded. "It's a fascinating place." She told Mrs. Kimball what she could about the several departments within the mill. She told her about how nice Lorraine Pringle was to her, and about Terry Sells and his gourmet picnic. She told her about everything she could remember about the people at the mill, partly to divert Mrs. Kimball's questions away from Max.

"I have some information for you, too," said Mrs. Kimball after a moment. "It's a good thing you're back now, because I've had a letter from the court, and I think you ought to go down with Mr. Black, my attorney. It's on Monday."

"Slow down," smiled Stephanie. "What's on Monday? What court? Tell me everything in plain English. What's this about a letter?"

"It's not really very important," said Mrs. Kimball, "but I thought you'd be interested since you know about the Carmichael estate personally. You see, everyone who ever had a claim on anything from Mr. Carmichael got the same letter. There is to be a hearing on Monday, and Mr. Black is going down as my representative."

"I thought all that property dispute was settled a long time ago," said Stephanie.

"It was. But there was a small matter I had forgotten about. Years ago, Judson had four or five acres way out in the woods near the railroad track. He let them lay idle. In fact, I suppose he forgot about them since they weren't much good for anything, and they weren't adjoining lots. So he didn't keep up the taxes on them, and according to state law, anyone who pays taxes on land like that— land that has no evident owner—is entitled to a deed to that land after so many years of keeping the taxes up. It's a sort of legal way to steal land, you might say—land that nobody else wants.

"Irwin Carmichael went to the title office and found a lot of land that hadn't been kept up by anyone, and he began to pay taxes on it. Well, Judson's four acres were among those. The thing is, if the owner shows up and resumes paying taxes on the land within a certain amount of time—about fifteen years, I think—the person who had acquired it in the meantime has to relinquish his claim to it.

"According to the title office, Judson is the owner of record, but Carmichael had paid taxes on the land for some ten years. So now I may have a claim on it if I want to pursue it.

"The fact is, I don't. The land is worthless, and since Carmichael paid taxes on it for so long, I think it ought to go to his heirs. Mr. Black is just going to make an appearance in court and give a statement to that effect. And I thought you might want to go along. I'm not going."

"Sure, I'd love to," said Stephanie.

"Mr. Black will be here at nine on Monday morning. Do you have any other plans?"

"No, I don't," replied Stephanie. Then she thought about the possibility of seeing Max in court, and almost regretted saying she would go. But it seemed to make her grandmother so happy for her to go that she resolved to stick it out.

Betsy fixed a huge country breakfast next morning—a Sunday morning ritual for as long as Stephanie could remember at her grandmother's house. When Betsy had cleared away, Stephanie and Mrs. Kimball sat with their coffee.

"I forgot to mention some other news last night," said Mrs. Kimball. "You remember the woman I told you about—Doreen? I don't know if you ever saw her?"

"No, I didn't. She must have come to Stanley after I went back to St. Louis."

"She's back in town. She evidently thinks she has a claim on Carmichael's inheritance."

"Oh, really? What do you think about it?"

"Not a chance." Mrs. Kimball wrinkled her brow. "I think it's pretty nervy of her even to show up."

"It takes all kinds of people to make a world, as you're so fond of saying, Grandmother."

". . . and I'm glad I'm not one of them," added Mrs. Kimball with a chuckle.

Stephanie called Nola, and Nola invited her for dinner. It was only Nola, Jeff, and Stephanie, and they had a marvelous dinner and a good time talking about Nola's and Jeff's plans. They were also excited to hear about Stephanie's experiences in Memphis, especially when Stephanie told them about Leon.

Jeff's eyes had been growing wider as Stephanie told him the tale, even though she omitted some of the more intimate and personal details. Jeff was indignant.

"He deserved the rough treatment by the police. They should have locked him up and thrown away the key."

"Well, it's over now," said Stephanie. "I'm glad to let sleeping dogs lie."

"Dog is right," said Jeff.

"Let's go sit in the back yard," said Nola. "The weather is so great, and it won't be long before we won't be able to enjoy it like this."

Nola had several lawn chairs under the trees near the barbecue pit. Just as they sat down, a car pulled up in the driveway by the side of the house.

"How nice," said Nola. "It's Marv and Janie." She whispered to Stephanie: "They've been squabbling off and on since you left for Memphis, and it's just because Janie is so head over heels in love with Marv. She's blindly jealous of him."

"Hi, folks," said Marv, as he and Janie came up. "Well, there's Stephanie, the St. Louis girl, back from the big city."

"I told you she wouldn't like it here," said Janie with a Raggedy Ann smile.

"I suppose you were right, Janie," said Stephanie, in her most winning manner. "I love the city. But I like it here, too. So peaceful."

Janie didn't have a comeback for that right away. She looked Stephanie over, and said, "I hear you have quite a romance going with Mr. Lamartine."

Stephanie was shocked. She remembered that in a small town like Stanley, word gets around fast. Janie would be blunt about it. Max's name had scarcely come up at dinner, and Stephanie had studiously avoided mentioning him. She saw Nola looking at her with a question on her face.

"You might say that, Janie," replied Stephanie as nonchalantly as she could, "but I think that's about over now. It just wouldn't work out."

Janie's face showed triumph.

"I'd prefer not to be continually fawning over some man," Stephanie added, "especially if he thought he was God's gift to women." She avoided looking at Marv.

"Oh, is that the way Mr. Lamartine is?" asked Janie.

"He impressed me as being quite modest and gentlemanly," put in Nola.

"He doesn't think he's God's gift to women," said Stephanie, "but a lot of other people do."

"Can't keep up with the competition, eh!" said Janie.

"You're not one to talk!" said Nola. Marv looked sheepish. "Besides, continued Nola, "there just wasn't any competition as far as I could tell. Especially when you consider that Max flew Stephanie to New Orleans for an evening on the town. But of course I don't know how it was in Memphis."

"I'll tell you in a few words," said Stephanie in a serious tone. "It was colder, life is at a more hectic pace, it's better in a lot of ways, not as good in some. Max is chairman of the board of a large textile mill—Lamartine Fabrics. He's a very important person in the industry, and he's busy all the time.

"I don't know how he was able to get away from his schedule to come down to take care of this legal business, but somehow he did. He has a lot on his mind, and he has a lot of problems. He has even more problems now, with Doreen Fletcher claiming some inheritance from his uncle's estate. Did you know about that, Nola?"

"I heard she was in town, and I figured that was why."

"She doesn't have the ghost of a chance, that I can see," said Stephanie. "But she's evidently going to give it a try."

"I vaguely remember that Mr. Lamartine's uncle was a sort of 'Goldfinger' type," said Janie, truly interested by now.

Stephanie blanched inwardly. She spoke half to herself: "Yes, he was. But I don't think Max is like that." She didn't add that she had been hoping against hope he wasn't.

"He doesn't seem to be anything like that to me," put in Jeff.

Nola noticed how uncomfortable Stephanie was. "I think we've said enough about Mr. Lamartine," she said. "Let's have something cool to drink." She went in the kitchen door to see what she could get for a snack.

Marv and Janie Left after having some lemonade with the others. Stephanie was a little heartened, because Janie seemed to be losing her antagonism toward her, and she attributed it to the relative coolness with which Marv treated her—owing, no doubt, to his guilt feelings about his less than mannerly performance at the dance.

"Do you want to talk about Max?" asked Nola, when Marv and Janie had gone. "It might help just to get it out in the open."

"Thanks, Nola. You're swell. But not right now. You probably noticed that it's—well, a little painful to me right now. Maybe we can get together some time soon." She glanced suggestively at Jeff, half across the yard, and Nola understood.

It wasn't yet dark yet when Stephanie drove home. On the way she passed Jerry Osgood's shack. Curiously, the front porch light wasn't on. The rest of the house was dark, and looking closer, she saw that the place was boarded up. The Osgoods were obviously gone.

Just a few yards on down the road Stephanie saw a boy walking along, barefoot, with hair the color of straw. He reminded Stephanie of Tom Sawyer, and appeared to be about nine or ten years old. On an impulse she stopped the car and got out.

"Hi there," she said. The boy gave a little wave of his hand.

"Do you live around here?" she asked.

"Yes'm. I live right over there." He pointed to the woods on the other side of the road, to a white house peeping through the trees, a house that Stephanie hadn't noticed before.

"I wonder if you know anything about the people who live here," she said, pointing to the Osgood's shack.

"Nobody lives there any more," he replied.

"What about Mr. Osgood?"

"Oh, those people?" He turned his head to look away from the shack out over the bean fields, newly ploughed.

Stephanie waited, and the boy started to whistle a little part of "My Bonny lies Over the Ocean."

"Did you say they didn't live there any more?"

"Yep."

"Do you know what happened to them?"

"Yep." He kicked a small rock with his foot, and resumed whistling.

Stephanie felt that her dialogue with the boy wasn't among the more rewarding conversations she had had. She persisted.

"Well, what did happen?"

"I saw the whole thing," he said, in a burst of effusion. "It was a big, black car came up and parked out on the road." He pointed with his hand. "Then this tall man got out and went in. I never saw a car like that. It must have been a Jag, or something. You wouldn't believe the shiny wheels. They would have knocked your eyes out. I'll bet that car would go a hundred and ten miles an hour in five seconds flat. I was sitting right over there in the bean row—there were bean rows over there last week. They just ploughed it yesterday. And that car was quiet, too. You couldn't even hear the motor running. You could hear the tires on the road, but you couldn't hear the motor. When he drove off that car was as quiet as a field mouse. And shiny! Whew! It was shinier than--Hey! You've got a pretty shiny car, too."

He kicked another rock with his foot. "What's your name, Ma'm?"

"My name's Stephanie. What's yours?"

"Dale."

"Glad to meet you, Dale."

"Say, I've got to go on home now." He started off, kicking pebbles.

"Wait, Dale. You haven't told me what happened to the Osgoods when that man went in."

"Oh." He made a wry face. "Nothing happened, they just left in their old truck. Took everything with them in a big barrel. Next day a man came out and nailed boards up on the windows and doors. Bye now." He ran across the highway toward the dirt road that ran by his own house.

It was that old fleeting vision of Max turning people out of their house, and it haunted Stephanie as she drove home.

Getting ready for bed that night, she couldn't keep her thoughts from wandering to Max. Why did she have to choose him, of all people, to fall in love with? And why was her love so strong, so all-consuming? Everything was against her in her love for him. As odious a creature as Jerry Osgood was, Max seemed to have little compunction about turning him and his father out of their home.

Max had said he gets what he wants. A shiver shook her frame when she thought of the way Max's touch evoked a sensual desire in her. She had to think of something else. Max was out of her reach now, but life still had to go on.

Nola. Nola and Jeff, how happy they would be together. And there were Marv and Janie. They had a rocky road, but she had noticed that Marv was paying more attention to Janie that he had before. Nola had told him how much Janie loved him, and he probably hadn't realized it until now. Further, he probably hadn't realized just how attractive Janie was.

That might be why she's spoiled, Stephanie thought, because she is so attractive her family has always given her everything. There were two boys in her family, one older than Jeff, but Janie was the only girl. Stephanie sighed. Young love!

How different my own situation is, she thought. In love with a man who doesn't even know I exist, and if he does it's only because he wants me for a sexual plaything—an easy woman. He had the gall to ask me to form a relationship with him just like Leon wanted. Even after his show of disgust at Leon's "proposition." I wonder if all men aren't alike.

She dreamed fitfully that Leon was chasing her, and Max was standing calm and self-assured. Leon looked even more like a cadaver than he had looked in the flesh. And Max had an enigmatic smile on his face—she couldn't tell if it was malicious or warm and understanding. The dream was like a ballet. Max stood in front of her while Leon ran at her. Suddenly Max held up his hand, ordering Leon to stop. Leon put his arm in front of his face and cried out: "Let me alone! Let me alone!"

Then Stephanie looked at him again and his face had undergone a transformation. It wasn't Leon's face any longer; it was the face of Jerry Osgood. Still he cried: "Let me alone! Let me alone!"

The dream woke Stephanie up, and she was unable to sleep again until she had gone down for a glass of milk, just as she had before.

In the morning Mr. Black pulled up in front of the house just as she was finishing her breakfast. Mrs. Kimball offered him coffee, but he said he didn't want to take the time. So Stephanie went with him in his car. He seemed to be a kindly man, graying around the temples.

"Do you know much about this situation, Stephanie?" he asked, more for conversation than for information.

"Only what Grandmother told me the other day. She said she doesn't want to try to claim that acreage.'

"No. In fact it would be more expensive to pay the back taxes and to bring up a claim in court than the property is worth. I think she's wise not to pursue it."

"What will happen to the lots?"

"They will revert to the estate, which is in the hands of Mr. Carmichael's nephew, Mr. Lamartine.

"I know Mr. Lamartine."

"Oh, you do? I didn't know his uncle. I just came to Stanley three years ago, and Carmichael's influence had waned by then. Your grandmother doesn't think much of him—Carmichael, I mean."

"No, she doesn't," said Stephanie with a grim laugh.

"But I understand Mr. Lamartine is a very fine young man. How do you know him?"

"I worked for him on the matter of the estate," she replied.

Mr. Black's ears pricked up. "Did you now? Then I suppose you know as much about the Carmichael probate as I do. There seem to be some real knotty problems concerning the inheritance, though I assume Mr. Lamartine is the only heir."

"Except for possibly Doreen Fletcher."

Mr. Black nodded. "I don't want to give an opinion, because I don't know all the facts, but as I see it she doesn't have a very good claim. But there are some precedents, and some strong ones, for her claim. So we'll have to wait and see."

The court of common pleas was on the second floor of the courthouse in Stanley. About two dozen people were seated in the chairs lining the walls of the large hall outside the hearing rooms, and Stephanie and Mr. Black joined them. A bailiff came out of one of the doors and announced that the hearings regarding the disposition of the property and claims made against that property of Mr. Irwin G. Carmichael, intestate, was now in progress.

The bailiff looked around. He called out: "Mr. Maximilian Lamartine."

"I'm Neils Patterson, attorney of record for Mr. Lamartine. I'll represent him," said the man who now came forward.

Stephanie had told herself that she didn't want to see Max, but still her heart sank to realize she wouldn't see him at all this morning. Nor probably ever again, she thought.

She had seen Neils Patterson in Memphis once, when he came in for a consultation with Max.

Now he was conservatively dressed in a medium brown suit. With his sandy hair and black-rimmed glasses, he looked the part of a successful corporate lawyer.

Stephanie glanced around the room. Some of the petitioners had evidently just come off the farm, while others looked like out-of-towners. One woman gave the impression that she looked down her nose at everyone. She was not large in stature—in fact she was rather slight, but her imposing manner made her seem larger than life. She stood rather than sat. She wore what could only be called a costume, a rich brocade skirt with a black lace blouse. Her hair was black, but was interspersed with gray, which gave it an almost other-worldly look Her whole outfit and her hawk-like eyes, studiously ignoring everything around her, suggested the word gypsy—gypsy in the noblest sense—to Stephanie, who judged the woman to be in her late fifties.

Stephanie noted the woman's aspect, and somehow she felt almost a bond of kinship with her. At that moment the bailiff called out: "Doreen Fletcher," and the woman drew herself up to her full height and said in a quiet voice, "I am Doreen Fletcher."

The bailiff beckoned for her to follow him into the hearing room. As she did so Stephanie felt her eyes rest on her for an instant, as they rested on everyone else in the hall.

Doreen Fletcher had become almost a fairy tale to Stephanie, someone on a level with Lily Langtry, and Stephanie could hardly believe in her existence. But here she was in the courthouse, denying her mythic nature by her very presence. Stephanie wanted to pinch herself to make sure of reality.

After an interminable interval, the door to the hearing room burst open and Doreen Fletcher emerged. A vacant look was on her face and in her eyes, and she entered the hall with a dramatic sweeping gesture. She had lost her bid for any part of Carmichael's inheritance. The hall was hushed.

Doreen's eyes dwelt on Stephanie for a long moment. In that look Doreen summed up her life, her world—grandiose schemes, passions, futility, heartbreak. That glance was a window into a life that remained a closed book to Stephanie.

No one else noticed the brief interchange of glances between Doreen and Stephanie. With the same flair as before, Doreen left the hall. After a few minutes, the bailiff reappeared and called: "Mrs. Eleanor Kimball."

Mr. Black answered for Mrs. Kimball, and he and Stephanie went into the hearing room. His statement only took a few minutes, and then Stephanie found herself walking back to Mr. Black's car with him.

"That was relatively painless," observed Mr. Black. "Interesting, though, wasn't it?"

Stephanie knew he was thinking of Doreen's appearance, as she was, but they both avoided speaking of her.

The rest of the day was gray, and it affected Stephanie considerable. She moped around the house, starting up when the telephone rang. Once it was Nola, but Stephanie put her off, saying she just wasn't feeling quite up to doing anything.

She had a light supper and decided to go to bed shortly after dusk. Her grandmother tried to draw her out, but Stephanie couldn't bring herself to be communicative. Even her own bedroom, with all its associations and memories, seemed lackluster for some reason.

Tuesday morning the weather had cleared. About noon Nola called.

"I've been hoping we could get together," she said. "How about meeting me in town when I get off work and we can do some shopping together? Maybe have a bite to eat, just the two of us."

Stephanie knew that shopping with Nola meant wandering around the stores in the mall and those that were open late downtown. "Sounds like fun," she said. "I need something to pick me up."

Nola was looking for a sweater, and they went in her car out to the mall, about five minutes out of town. They hit almost every store in the mall.

None of the stores in the mall seemed to have exactly the right thing. Finally, a little after six they sat down at a pizzateria.

"It doesn't look like you're having any luck, does it?" suggested Stephanie.

"Not in finding my sweater. But I am having a little luck in another way, because I've managed to bring you out of your blue mood. It's Max, isn't it?"

Stephanie looked helpless. "Yes, it is. I didn't want to bring my troubles to you, but I suppose you're the only person I have who can come anywhere close to understanding the way I feel."

"I don't know if I can or not."

"Yes, you can. You're in love, just like I am."

Nola put her hand across the table to pat Stephanie's. "I knew you had fallen for Max. You two just seemed pretty well matched."

"I don't know how well matched we seemed, but I know . . ."

"You and he—became lovers, didn't you?"

"If you want to put it that way, yes. Oh, Nola," she squeezed her friend's hand, "I don't know how I can live without him."

"Well, don't try. Go to him. Does he know how you feel? Have you told him?"

"It's more complicated than that. He wants me to become his mistress."

"His mistress? Did he actually ask you that?"

"Yes. Well, not really. I didn't give him the chance. But that's what he wanted, and I told him . . . that I didn't love him, that it was only sexual."

Nola sighed.

"I know he wouldn't want me for long, anyway," continued Stephanie. "And on top of that, he's following right in his uncle's footsteps."

"His uncle's footsteps? What are you talking about?"

"You know he's Irwin Carmichael's nephew."

"By marriage only. I knew that. Besides that, I have an idea that Irwin Carmichael wasn't as bad as you make him out."

"Now listen to this, Nola. You know, and I know, that Jerry Osgood is a real low-life. But just because the man is a low-life doesn't mean he ought to be turned out of his home."

"Max did that?"

Stephanie nodded. "Turned him and his old father out. God knows where they went."

"But maybe . . . there's some sort of an explanation."

"I don't know. But I know I just couldn't put myself in Max's hands, like a slave. You know how weak-willed women often do that for the men they idolize, and it brings them nothing but despair and hopelessness. That's exactly what he wanted, for me to become his slave, and when he was tired of me he would have turned me out—just like he turned the Osgoods out. And he would have found somebody else to take my place. That's why I told him I didn't love him."

"But if you do love him, and love him like I think you do . . ." Nola broke off. She looked at her friend. She knew how brave Stephanie was, but she also knew that Stephanie was right, it could lead to an empty life and to despair, if Max were the kind of man Stephanie had suggested.

"That's just it," said Stephanie. "I do love him like that. And I'm going crazy because of it."

"I may not have the answer for you," said Nola. "And I don't know whether you want my advice or not."

"I don't have to take it, do I? But it sure might help if you had a suggestion. Tell me something, Nola, tell me anything. God knows I can't go on like this."

"You're in love with him, right?" said Nola. "And you don't think he loves you. Well, Stephanie, you might be wrong about that. He might love you just as much as you love him."

"Then why hasn't he told me so?"

"I don't know. I don't have any idea why men act the way they do. But still it's a possibility."

"Remote."

"Then, dammit, if you think he doesn't love you, the only thing you can do is try to forget him. If he does love you, then he'll let you know."

Stephanie was silent. I've effectively prevented that, she thought. "I came right out and told him I didn't love him—he'd be a fool to keep trying."

"Hey," said Nola, "there are other fish in the sea. Millions. And a sharp girl like you won't ever have any trouble getting them on your line."

"That's the trouble—I don't want any other fish. I only want Max."

"Then it looks like it all comes down to the same old solution. You're going to have to swallow your pride. I hate to say it, but if you can't forget him then you'll have to go to him. You'll just have to take whatever he dishes out."

"And let him walk all over me?"

"Look, Stephanie, aren't you assuming a lot? Did he actually say he didn't love you?"

"No, but . . ."

"Did he say he wanted you to . . . live with him?"

"Well, no . . ."

"One more thing. What about this Osgood business? You said he turned them out of their house."

"The way I heard it, he drove up and went in, and while he was there, they packed up everything they had, and left. You know the place is boarded up now. Well, Max did that."

"Maybe they didn't pay their rent," said Nola. "Or maybe he was doing it because of you—did you ever think of that? Osgood didn't act like much of a gentleman to you, and—of course it's only conjecture, but if Max loved you, wouldn't he want to get back at the man who treated you so badly?"

"Nola, I don't want anybody—even the man I love—to treat people like that because of me."

"You mean, especially the man you love. I know how you feel. But there has to be an explanation."

"Such as organized crime techniques. I'm surprised he didn't fit Osgood with cement boots for a little swim in the Mississippi!"

Nola laughed a grim laugh. "Oh, Stephanie, cut it out. You're imagining things."

"Food for thought," said Stephanie with a little grin. "Speaking of food, we had better do something about these open-face sandwiches before they get cold."

She was feeling better, and Nola was glad to see she had a healthy appetite. The shopping trip wasn't a total loss, even though Nola didn't find the sweater she was looking for.

Stephanie slept well that night, and was able to face the morning with a more purposeful attitude than she'd had since leaving Memphis, even though she hadn't decided what she ought to do yet.

Betsy and Mrs. Kimball both knew she was having a difficult time. Mrs. Kimball didn't want to interfere. She knew that if Stephanie wanted her advice, she would ask, and if she gave it unasked, then it wouldn't be advice, it would be meddling.

But at breakfast she couldn't help asking: "You haven't heard from Mr. Lamartine this week, have you?"

Stephanie trembled slightly at hearing his name unexpectedly. "No, I haven't" she replied in a cool manner. "Our business is done, and he has no reason to contact me."

"No reason?"

Stephanie ignored Mrs. Kimball's probing question, and pretended to be involved with her breakfast.

She idled away her time in her bedroom after the meal. Lunch was a haphazard affair, and after lunch she went up to her grandmother in the living room.

"Grandmother," she said, "I'm going for a little drive in the country."

Mrs. Kimball was immediately attentive. She knew Stephanie was having a difficult time, and Stephanie had always been one to work out her own problems in her own way.

"I just thought I'd tell you so you don't worry about me," said Stephanie. "I—I've been having some . . . personal problems I have to think out, and . . ."

"Is it anything you'd care to talk to me about, child?"

"Not just now, Grandmother. I do want to talk to you about it, but not right now. Maybe later."

"How long do you expect to be gone?"

"I thought I'd drive out the country roads and look at the scenery. I don't know how long I'll be gone—probably most of the day. Don't wait dinner for me if I'm not back. I'll be able to manage."

"You know there aren't any fast-food places out in the country. Not any people, either. It depends on where you go, you might see nothing but swamp critters."

Stephanie laughed at her grandmother's homespun manner. It put them a little closer together. She gave her grandmother a little hug.

"Don't you worry about me; I'll be all right, Grandmother. I promise I'll be careful."

Following an old family tradition, she blew her grandmother a little kiss as she went out the door.

"Don't drive fast, Stephanie," called Mrs. Kimball.

Nine

Max

Stephanie stopped at the service station on the highway, the same place she had first seen Max. The same attendant was there, and Stephanie decided not to be impatient with him. She knew he would finally finish filling her car with gas, and resume his lounging position in his chair to contemplate the field across the highway, pausing now and then in his meditations to remove his billed cap and scratch his head.

She had the rest of the day before her, and she knew her grandmother wouldn't worry even if she didn't appear again until after dinnertime. So she drove leisurely through the countryside, aimlessly, neither knowing nor caring where she went or how far. She knew she wouldn't be hungry, not physically. But there was a hunger she couldn't satisfy, a hunger not of the body but of the soul, and as she drove mile after mile along the winding country roads she began to realize that this hunger was threatening to consume her—it was a longing that finally took shape and form, and the object of this overwhelming longing and yearning was Max.

She went over everything she could recall about Max, every detail about every contact she had had with him. Each moment was vivid in her mind, and she could feel every touch of his hand, feel his breath on her cheek, feel his skin as they lay together during those too brief, too blissful moments. Every intonation of his voice, every position and posture of his head and body as they walked, talked, sat, and lay together—she could almost relive those experiences as if they weren't governed by time, place, or situation.

What had she done wrong? Everything. If only she hadn't gone to work for him, helping him with that mess of an inheritance. If only she hadn't gone to Memphis. If only she hadn't gone to dinner with him in New Orleans. The list of "if onlies" grew longer.

But if she hadn't done all that, she would never have experienced the thrill of hearing him whisper words of love to her. She would never have realized how that current that passed between them could grow into a sensation that enveloped her entire body, a sensation, a fulfillment that she could only realize with Max.

On the other hand, she had driven him away from her, just as sure as if she had told him off in a grand "scene." What was it he had asked? It was as vivid as everything else in their relationship to Stephanie: "I want to be your only lover," were his words. She would never forget them.

She should have thrown caution to the wind, should have said that it was what she wanted too, because it was. But what had she replied? She had given him the only reply possible. If she had said yes, yes, I want to be your lover—the most profound wish of her existence—what would he have done? He would have done as all men would do. Leon showed that. He would have "kept" her. Kept her for his convenience—"convenience" was the only word to describe it.

So she told him a lie. It was a lie that was justified in her mind at the time. But it was a lie she couldn't confess, even to Nola. Nola would have thought her mad to refuse Max, even to refuse to be his mistress. The lie was to keep that from happening. As abruptly as possible, she had effectively terminated their relationship by saying that she didn't want him, that she was only attracted to him physically, that she didn't love him. It had turned the tables on him and had guaranteed that he wouldn't try to reestablish contact with her. Oh, she would get a check from him for the work she did, but it would be a cold, impersonal check, probably written by Lorraine on the check-writing machine at the mill. And he would forget her. In fact, she thought, in all likelihood he had forgotten about her even now, as she drove along the seemingly endless country roads north of Stanley, trying to make some sense, some reason out of her future without Max.

Nola had been sympathetic, but she couldn't know the depth of Stephanie's feeling for Max. She had said to try to forget him. But Stephanie knew that was impossible. There was a constant ache in her body that was intensified whenever she thought of him.

It was hard to know about Max's uncle. Everything she had heard about him was negative. But for some reason, that encounter with Doreen Fletcher at the courthouse had put a completely different aspect on Stephanie's feelings about Irwin Carmichael. Call it an intuition, call it sixth sense, call it anything, but there was a kindred light in those eyes that flickered on her that instant in the hall of the courthouse, a light that seemed to tell Stephanie more about Irwin Carmichael than she could have ever learned from any other source.

She had formed her entire opinion of Max long before that moment of contact with Doreen Fletcher's probing eyes. She had formed it almost solely on the basis of his relationship to Irwin Carmichael, and he wasn't even related to him except by marriage! A flimsy reason to suspect someone's integrity. And perhaps she had only been rationalizing; rationalizing because he struck awe in her, frightened her. Maybe she had a premonition that she would fall in love with him, and she was afraid to fall in love—with him or with anyone, after her experience with Leon.

Looking back, Stephanie realized that everything she found out about Max had accumulated to paint a picture of him that could hardly have been true. First she found out he was Irwin Carmichael's nephew. Then she found that he was wealthy, and had assumed that he had become wealthy at the expense of others. Then she was led to believe that he was cruel, because of the way he treated the Osgoods. And Marla O'Neal—her relationship to him cast a cloud over him in Stephanie's eyes. Finally, he had wanted her to be his mistress.

And it was this last factor that had led her to reject him. She might have dealt with all the others except the last—she couldn't compromise herself in that way, not when the incident with Leon was so fresh, so real, and so disgusting!

She realized that she was racing along the country road, and took her foot off the accelerator—she had promised her grandmother she would drive carefully. At that moment, she heard a tremendous noise overhead. It sounded like a thousand eagles batting their wings, and Stephanie was brought forcibly to the present. She finally identified the sound: a helicopter. Just as she realized what it was, she saw it directly in front of her car, swooping low. It landed in the middle of the road, not three hundred yards away, and Stephanie was forced to stop the car. She thought it must be someone mad, to land right in the middle of the road, but there it was and a man had jumped out and was running toward her car. Max!

He came up to the car in a few steps. "Move on over," he said, over the roar of the helicopter. "I'll drive."

Stephanie had no will power left. "Max, Max." Weakly she muttered his name as she undid her seat belt and slid over to the passenger side. In a daze she saw the helicopter, with Eric Hammond at the controls, lift off the ground. Max pulled the car into a sandy road that intersected the small highway.

"That was a fool thing to do," said Stephanie between her teeth.

"You know, it wasn't easy to find you in this maze of side roads, dirt roads, and highways," he said, looking at her out of the corner of his eye. "You could have been thoroughly lost."

Stephanie was still confused, and in her confusion she detected a tone of possessiveness in his voice. She was stubbornly resisting the impulse to melt into his arms. Instead she compressed her lips into a pout and crossed her arms on her chest.

"What do you want?" she asked.

Max took a deep breath. He didn't answer her question, but slowed the car on the irregular sandy surface of the road and glanced over at her. She was a small bundle in the corner of the car.

He stopped the car. "Well, don't you think it was a little cheeky, running out on me like you did?" he asked. "Lorraine said she didn't know what to tell you, and that you gave her a brief goodbye and cleared out. Without so much as a note of farewell or a 'kiss my foot' to me."

"I told you how I felt!"

"You lied to me!"

Stephanie had been watching her chance, and she quickly reached over and yanked the key out of the ignition. She undid her seat belt and opened the door and leapt out almost into the cotton bushes growing in the field. The bushes were nearly chest high, and Stephanie ran, darting here and there among the bushes, confused and aimlessly trying to escape from this man who had caused such an upheaval in her life.

Max was effectively surprised. He jumped out on the driver's side, and as Stephanie looked back she saw him gaining on her. She crouched behind the cotton bushes to conceal herself. Just ahead she spied a thicket of trees and undergrowth, and figured if she could gain that thicket she could lose him.

She peeked out between the bushes, but Max was nowhere to be seen. Gathering her strength, she mad a dash for the thicket.

Then it was all over. Max appeared from nowhere to cut her off from the safety of the tangled growth. He caught her by the arms, and she lunged, upsetting his balance and sending them both toppling onto the grassy soil between the neglected cotton bushes near the thicket.

"Max, Max" she muttered between her teeth, and then her words were stifled by the warmth of his lips, insistent, demanding. Feverishly she clung to him. All her desire for him was telescoped into those impetuous moments. Over and over he whispered her name as he pulled her sweater-coat off her and loosened her blouse.

In the cotton field, with only the sparse grass and her sweater for their bed, they made love. It was frantic, it was savage, but it was beautiful. To Stephanie there seemed an urgency about their lovemaking, as if there would be no tomorrow, or worse, as if tomorrow Max would be gone out of her life forever. She had no way to know whether she would ever see this man again, this half-barbaric man whose very touch infused her with excitement.

Furiously, but skillfully and deliberately he tore at her clothes, and she thrilled when he explored her body with his hands and lips. He inflamed her with a rising desire and passion until he sent her almost into oblivion by the ecstasy of their love.

A long time afterward Stephanie became aware of the gladsome sound of doves in the nearby thicket, secret sharers of their fulfillment. Her head was cradled on Max's arm, and he was silently looking up at the darkening sky.

Suddenly Stephanie sat up. "We can't do this!" she said in anxiety. "I can't give myself to you, not now or any other time."

"It's too late," he said simply. His eyes were smiling.

"But Max, I can't commit myself to you, and I certainly don't want an occasional fling." She spat the words out sarcastically.

"You must," he said in an even tone. "It's inevitable. In fact you are committed to me, just as sure as those doves over in the woods are committed to one another. There's no way out now. I told you I get what I want, and it's you I want."

She was dressing as neatly as she could under the circumstances. Impetuously she stabbed her arms into the sleeves of the sweater.

"You don't want me," she said. "I told you before, and I'll tell you again, I don't . . . love you." She had intended to hurl the words at him, but she found that her sentence had trailed off for lack of conviction.

"Come along," he said, "we'll talk about it later. Where's the car key?"

Stephanie stood open-mouthed. She had been in such a hurry to get away from Max that she couldn't remember what had happened to the key. She looked at Max, he looked at her, and suddenly they both burst out laughing.

"Isn't this a pretty mess," he said. "Here we are, miles from any civilization, with a perfectly fine car, and we can't make it run for lack of a key." He laughed again.

"We'd better start looking for it before it gets too dark to see," he went on. "Let's try to retrace your steps."

With Stephanie in the lead, they searched the ground along the same path she had taken in her mad dash, as well as they were able. She had taken a zigzag path, and their search was fruitless. They combed the cotton field until it was almost dark, and then came up to lean on the side of the car, arms around one another.

"I suppose we're stuck here together," she said. She put her arms tightly around Max, needing his strength.

"I suppose so," he said. He held her close. It was comforting to be in his arms, and she didn't care what happened to her as long as he held her like this.

They looked into one another's eyes, and Stephanie saw a smile creeping into his face.

"I have to confess," he said, reaching into his pocket, "I found the key just now, right here beside the car."

"You! You seducer." They both laughed and he held the door for her. It was just getting dark, but the moon was almost full.

"Max, I'm afraid we're lost. I don't have GPS, and I don't have any idea where we are—I didn't have any plan to my driving, I just drove."

"You silly goose," he returned. "You don't think Eric and I could circle this whole area for over an hour without figuring out where we were, do you?" He chuckled.

"What were you and he doing here, flying over these fields in the first place?" She was totally confused.

He pulled the car into the highway. "Don't you realize it by now? I told you before, I need you, and I can't just let you walk—or rather run—out of my life."

He was silent for a moment. "I know you think a lot of things about me that just aren't true," he continued. "Maybe some of them are. But I don't think I'm quite the bad guy you believe me to be."

Stephanie remained silent. She was afraid he could hear her heart beating, in her confused state of emotions. She remembered vividly what Nola had said about Max, that if he loved her he would let her know.

"I know you think I'm just like my uncle Irwin," he was saying. "But you've got to believe me, I'm not. He was only my uncle by marriage, and you can take it from me, my aunt Estelle knew she had made a mistake by marrying him. Oh, she paid for it, paid dearly. But that's all in the past. Everybody knows he was a swindler and a cheat. Even Doreen Fletcher knew it. She was the only one who was able to do anything about it. She tapped into a lot of his hidden resources, just like you said."

"I saw her at court," said Stephanie. "Monday. The day she lost her claim."

"Obviously there's a lot you don't know about this case, Stephanie, even as closely as you worked with me on it. And there's a lot you don't know about me. The fact is, she didn't really lose her claim."

Stephanie looked up at Max. "Yes, she did. I saw her leave the court-room."

"Look. Her claim was only for one of his houses, and yes, legally she lost the claim to the house. But Stephanie, I'm selling it to her—a private deal."

"You are? I don't understand."

"She has a beauty operator's license. She's opening a beauty shop in that house, probably by the end of the month."

"How much did you sell her the house for?"

"Five hundred dollars."

Stephanie was dumbfounded. "I can't believe it," she said.

"You see, I'm not such an ogre. I can be nice even to people who appear to be my enemies."

The name Jerry Osgood flashed through Stephanie's mind, and she smirked.

Max appeared to read her mind. "Even to Jerry Osgood," he said.

"To Jerry Osgood?" Stephanie remembered the conversation with the boy named Dale. She had a mental image of Max turning the Osgoods out of the shack.

Max sighed. "I tried everything I could to help him and his father. But he's the kind who just won't be helped."

Stephanie gritted her teeth. "I know how you helped him," she muttered.

"Do you?"

"Yes. I know you turned him and his old father out of that shack."

"Then you might also know they signed a contract to work the land for me over a year ago, and to date they haven't planted the first seed. And you probably know they took the shack rent free, with the understanding that they would fix it up, and they were to get twenty percent of the profits from the crops, and the only thing they did to the house, in the way of improvement, was to put a light bulb on the porch."

Stephanie was amazed. But still she had that awful picture in her mind of the Osgoods leaving the shack with a barrel full of their belongings.

"But Max," she said. "They are human beings, after all! I know how you turned them out."

"Then you've probably heard that I've put the old man—who actually is harmless—in a rest home, and that I gave Jerry a hundred dollars when he left—something to get started on, and probably the most money he's ever seen in his life."

"Max! I can't believe it. I don't know what to say."

"You don't have to say anything."

The small bundle that was Stephanie crept a little closer to Max. "Max, forgive me."

"For what? You haven't done anything to be forgiven for."

"No, but I've thought badly of you. I've thought that you were . . . cruel."

He lowered his brows and darted her little looks. "I am cruel," he said in his samurai accent. "And I eat young women. Roast them and eat them for dinner!"

Stephanie tried to suppress her laughter, but she couldn't resist his drollery.

She leaned on his shoulder as he drove. She felt it was a stolen hour. So Max wasn't the person she had thought him to be. She knew she couldn't become what he wanted, though. But how could she say it?

"Max," she said, "I want to thank you for everything you've done for me. But you know it won't work for us. I just can't bring myself to be what you want me to be."

"And what do you think I want you to be, my pretty maid?" His tone was intended to put her at her ease, but it only made what she had to say more difficult.

"I know what you want. You want to share . . ." She broke off. She was silent for a moment, choked with emotion. Then she resumed: "You want to share with me what we just shared, back there in the cotton field, at your own convenience. And I can't do it."

"What about yourself? Are you trying to tell me you don't have any feelings for me at all?"

"No, no. Of course I do. I just can't see myself as a . . . kept woman."

They were just turning onto the small highway to her grandmother's house, and Max squealed the brakes to a halt.

"A kept woman? What are you talking about? Dammit, Stephanie, that's not what I want. I want you to be my wife, and I won't take no for an answer. I love you more than I imagined I could ever love anyone. Even if you don't love me. Maybe you can learn to love me, as they say in the movies."

A flood of emotion swept over Stephanie. "But you didn't say marriage. I didn't know . . ." She was too choked up to go on.

Deliberately he pulled the car into the road again. "Of course I didn't say marriage. You told me flat out that you didn't love me. I didn't think I had a chance."

She had said she didn't love him. And it would be almost impossible to say anything else, now. A little tear trickled from her eye. She drew away from him. Still those doubts were creeping into her mind, doubts about his motives, doubts about his relationship with other women. She felt she had to be sure about him, even if there was no way she could convince him now that she actually did love him.

He turned into the driveway at Mrs. Kimball's house.

Ten

Future

It was with mixed emotions that Stephanie walked with Max into the house. What could she possibly say to her grandmother? Mrs. Kimball had probably guessed the cause of Stephanie's turmoil—had undoubtedly guessed. But Stephanie hadn't been able as yet to say to Max that she really loved him, even though it was true, so true that it was crying to be let out.

She felt caught in an impossible situation.

"Stephanie, come in, child," said Mrs. Kimball, when they entered the foyer. "Bring that young man in here too. I want to take a good look at him.

"Why hello, Mr. Lamartine. It's quite an honor to have you here. You have done so much for us; I feel I owe you a lot."

"Please, Mrs. Kimball," replied Max, "just call me Max. And you shouldn't feel that way, I only did what I thought was the right thing."

"Will somebody please let me in on the secret?" said Stephanie. "I seem to have stumbled right into the middle of a mystery story where everybody knows the solution except me."

"No mystery, really," said Max. "It's nothing very important . . ."

"Oh, yes it is," said Ms. Kimball. "Here, just a minute and I'll let you see for yourself, Stephanie." She rolled her chair over to a small drum table and took a letter from the drawer.

"This came in the afternoon's mail," she said. "Just take a look at it."

It was a letter from Neils Patterson, a form letter addressed to all the petitioners for property in the probate case of Irwin Carmichael. It stated that "the accompanying check in the amount of [blank] represents the current market value of the property in question." The blank was filled in with $42,000. It was for the property Mr. Black had gone to court about, the four acres in the woods near the railroad track. The letter further stated that the same property was offered for sale at the same current market value, and that if the receiver wished to buy back the property, all that was required was an endorsement of the check. If the receiver didn't wish to exercise this option, the property would go on the open market. Neils Patterson signed the letter as attorney for Maximilian Lamartine, heir to the estate of Irwin Carmichael, deceased.

Stephanie stared at the letter. So that was the purpose of the assessments she had solicited from the land office, and the title searches. Max was systematically making what restitution he could for his uncle's wrongdoing all along, and Stephanie didn't know it. He never talked about himself, never tried to take credit for what he actually did.

Suddenly Stephanie realized that she had judged Max too bitterly and too harshly all this time. She had failed to recognize what kind of man he was, but instead had prejudged him.

She knew she had to speak, had to beg his forgiveness, had to tell him how she felt about him. But the words wouldn't come—she didn't know how to say it. Mrs. Kimball saw that Stephanie was at a loss for words.

"When I talked to Max today," said Mrs. Kimball, "I tried to tell him . . ."

Stephanie interrupted her grandmother. "You talked to him today?" She looked from her grandmother to Max and back again.

"Yes." Mrs. Kimball looked at Max. "Maybe you should tell her about your phone call."

"You see," said Max, "I had to be in Canada over the weekend. When I got back to Memphis late yesterday, Lorraine told me you had gone. So this afternoon I called here, and Mrs. Kimball said you had gone driving out in the countryside, and I suspected you might have gone up in a northerly direction. The logical way to find you was by helicopter."

"But why did you have to find me?" Stephanie felt that at any moment her eyes would be filled with tears, and she tried to hold them back.

"If you'll excuse me," interjected Mrs. Kimball, "I think Betsy needs me in the kitchen." She wheeled herself out of the room.

"I hope you know what a fine lady your grandmother is," said Max.

"I certainly do. But you're evading the issue, Mr. Lamartine. Why did you have to find me today? Or any time? Weren't you able to find comfort in Marla O'Neal's arms, or someone else's?"

"Now Stephanie, is that fair? I had to find you because your grandmother told me . . . well, something about how you felt about me. Besides that, you don't know anything about my relationship with Marla."

"Why don't you tell me, then?"

Max sighed. "All right. But you'll have to promise not to ask any more questions about her. Deal?"

"Deal."

"Well, it was only one of those casual flings, as you would call it. I was in New Orleans in the spring about three years ago, and I just sort of bumped into her during Mardi Gras.

"She needed help, Stephanie, needed it badly. She had a little apartment near the French Quarter. She was into alcohol pretty heavily, and I helped her break away from that.

"There was never anything serious about our relationship, certainly not on my part, and she knew it, but I suspect she didn't feel the same way. We didn't have any caustic words when we parted—it just wasn't that sort of friendship—but I think she felt that something should have come of it, marriage, or a long-term relationship, or something. She was voice student, and I helped her get into the conservatory.

"Yes, we did have a grand time at the Mardi Gras, but that was really the high point of our relationship. Since then we have remained good friends, but I've only seen her occasionally, and then only by chance.

"I didn't know she was singing at Treasure Cove. If I had, well, maybe I wouldn't have taken you there."

"So she was your protégé and your lover."

"We made a deal, Stephanie, remember? No more questions."

"All right."

Max was sitting on the edge of the sofa, and he took her wrist to pull her down beside him. "About today, there's a good explanation," he said.

"I'm all ears."

"Stephanie, maybe this isn't the time or the place to tell you. But I have to tell you anyway. I've thought about it a long time, and there's only one conclusion I can draw."

"You've thought about what?" she interrupted.

He held up his hand. "Hold on," he said. "I want to go through this my own way. I've thought about what you told me, remember that night at your apartment? You said you didn't love me."

Stephanie's face was a mask.

"I finally figured out that you must have been lying. Your grandmother indicated the same thing by what she said. But God only knows why you would have lied to me."

She closed her eyes and tried to conceal her emotional reaction.

"And when I had that piece to the puzzle," he continued, "I had to see you. It's as simple as that. When I called here, your grandmother told me some things, things I would never have suspected or hoped."

"Like what?"

"She knew from the way you've been acting that something was bothering you. And she said your friend Nola had called here for you. Since you keep your cell phone turned off."

"Nola?"

"Nola was evidently very concerned about you. She told your grandmother that she was actually afraid for you to be out driving alone."

"Humph."

"Yes, I know you can take care of yourself. But Nola told your grandmother that you and she had had a long talk, and she said that . . . well, she said you loved me. I had lost all hope of ever hearing that. I took you at your word when you said you didn't, but now your grandmother was telling me the one thing I had hoped and longed to hear."

Stephanie put her head on his shoulder. Then she looked into his eyes. "It's true, Max. I love you as I love my very breath and life."

He held her close. After a long moment of joy in one another's embrace, free and without reservations or inhibitions, he began to whisper again: "Stephanie, ever since I first saw you at the service station—do you remember?—I've had you in my dreams. You've been a constant part of my every day, every moment. I told you that I get what I want. It's you I want, not just for weekends, or some such foolishness, but every minute of every day. Will you? Will you be my own, my wife?"

"Oh, yes, Max, yes. It's all I ever dreamed of. If you only knew how hard it was for me to tell you <u>no</u> that night, to send you away from me . . ."

"Why did you? Why did you say you didn't love me? You can't imagine what a blow that was to me."

"I was a fool, Max. I caused myself as much misery as I caused you. It was just a complication, an accumulation of so many things. And coming right on top of that horrid scene with Leon . . . that's what I thought you wanted, too. I thought you wanted a plaything, a mistress, just like Leon. Everything I had found out about you had convinced me that you were a cruel louse, a blackguard—a desirable blackguard, but a blackguard just the same. I didn't know you were the beautiful, tender person you are."

"So you thought I wasn't on the up and up, and that I was something of a rat?"

"All the evidence was there. I guess it was the misdeeds of your uncle that started it all off. But we've been over all that, and I want to beg your forgiveness. Max, I'm so happy."

Max wiped away the tears, tears of joy, from her cheeks.

"I hate to interrupt this tender scene," said Mrs. Kimball from the door. "I thought you both might be hungry, so Betsy and I have made same scrambled eggs with toast and hot cocoa. It won't stay hot for long."

Arm in arm Stephanie and Max made their way into the dining room. Only when they sat down did they realize how famished they both were, and they ate the delicious food heartily. They spoke little during the meal, but cast many glances in one another's direction. As they sat over their second cup of cocoa, Mrs. Kimball came in from the kitchen.

"Max, you'll sleep in the spare room next to the kitchen. Lights are usually out by ten here, but tonight I may make an exception." A twinkle was in her eye.

"Oh, Mrs. Kimball, you mustn't go to any trouble," began Max.

"Nonsense, young man. I'll hear no more about it. Stephanie can show you where everything is."

And the matter was settled. Still Mrs. Kimball waited at the door as if expecting Stephanie to say something.

"Oh, grandmother," Stephanie burst out, "we—we're going to be married!" She could hardly hold the tears back again.

Mrs. Kimball smiled. "Wonderful! Congratulations to you both. I consider myself to be the lucky one, to have a young man like you for a future grandson. Now just how long has this been going on?" She narrowed her eyes in mock suspicion.

"Go along with you, Grandmother. As if you didn't know. Max only asked me a few minutes ago in the living room, but you knew what was going on."

Mrs. Kimball assumed a sterner expression. "Just remember, I'm breaking the rules of the house for you two, but just this once. Goodnight." And she wheeled out with a flourish. Moments later Stephanie and Max heard the faint clank of the elevator.

Stephanie led Max back into the living room. This time, as they sat together on the sofa, it was Stephanie who first found his lips. She was in the arms of the man she loved, and she knew he loved her. His lips were demanding, and as he held her close she knew nothing—not her foolish notions, not even the ghost of Irwin Carmichael—nothing would ever come between them again.

Her eyes were dry by this time, and she felt she could carry on an intelligent conversation. "So it was Nola. She told Grandmother. She let the cat out of the bag."

"That's what your grandmother says. But I'll tell you, I wouldn't be surprised if Mrs. Kimball had it figured out all along."

"No doubt about it. She—"

He stifled her words with his lips on hers. "We have a future to plan for," he whispered.